# CHRISTMAS FICTION OFF THE BEATEN PATH

## A Christmas Anthology of Inspirational Stories

***Special Hardcover Edition***
***with recipes, Christmas memories, traditions, and stories.***

**Mt Zion Ridge Press**
**Books Off the Beaten Path**

***www.MtZionRidgePress.com***

Mt Zion Ridge Press LLC
295 Gum Springs Rd, NW
Georgetown, TN 37366

*https://www.mtzionridgepress.com*



ISBN 13: 978-1-955838-81-8

Published in the United States of America
Publication Date: November 1, 2023

Editor-In-Chief: Michelle Levigne
Executive Editor: Tamera Lynn Kraft
Editor: Jenna Kraft

# Table of Contents

# Mary, Did You Know?
## *By Patricia Meredith*

I couldn't tell him everything. That would have required baring my soul in a way that I just wasn't ready to do. So much had happened. So much was still to happen, I knew.

Luke sat across from me, his ink ready, his hand poised, the thin piece of parchment unrolled before him. He was ready to write down whatever I said. Whatever I remembered.

The trouble was, I remembered too much.

I remembered his smile. The way his eyes looked at me for the very first time. His first laugh. His first steps. The first time he wrote his name. The first time he whittled a bowl. The first time he stood up in synagogue to read from the Torah.

My hands were spotted, wrinkled, and stiff now, but I remembered it all. Every moment. I couldn't forget. I just couldn't. I'd never been able to, and I prayed I never would.

My baby boy, my sweet baby boy.

His face came to my mind. His face the last time I'd seen him…that I'd ever see him on this earth.

But I knew I'd see that face again.

"So, Mary," Luke said, "did you know your son would be the Messiah?"

<><><>

It had been just another ordinary day. It was my day to wash the laundry, so I was out pinning the wet clothes and blankets to the line when the angel appeared.

I'll never forget the sight, though it's difficult to describe. There was light and color and brightness and a form and a voice.

The best I can do is compare it to staring straight into the sun as it's setting, and those wiggly lines appear across your vision when you close your eyes. But this time my eyes were open, wide open, like they didn't want to even blink for fear of discovering it was all a dream.

I fell to the ground I was so surprised, my knees giving out completely as my heart thumped loud enough to be heard across the village. Then it spoke.

Its voice: like liquid honey pouring down a sore throat. Only I hadn't realized I was sick until that instant. I hadn't thought I needed that light in my life until he showed up and filled it.

And changed it forever.

Suddenly, I was pregnant. I knew it without question.

But I didn't tell Joseph, or my mother, and certainly not my father.

I just ran.

I ran to someone who I thought might be able to comfort me—she had before, and we were very close. I ran to my cousin, Elizabeth.

Now there was a surprise.

I walked into her home and gathered her in my arms, only to discover she, too, was pregnant—obviously so. She told me then of her own expected child, whom I'd felt leaping in her belly when we hugged.

But she had a husband. I did not.

Zechariah didn't say anything when I started to show—I knew he couldn't even if he'd wanted to, as Elizabeth had told me when I'd first arrived that God had taken away his voice for not believing—but I could see the disappointment in his eyes. I was betrothed to a wonderful man, whom I'd felt blessed to know would soon join me as my partner in life, but we were unmarried, nonetheless.

I hid with Elizabeth for three months. That was how long it took me to get up the courage to go back. She'd hidden for five months, she'd admitted, but I couldn't remain so long. A nudge in my soul told me it was time. Time to make the long walk home.

Time to tell Joseph.

<><><>

He didn't take it well.

Neither did my parents.

I'll be forever grateful to them for not throwing me out on the street. They wanted to believe me. I could tell. And they were there when I told Joseph, so they saw the surprised look on his face—a look that wouldn't have been there if I'd been lying. I think, in a way, it helped them realize I was telling the truth.

Joseph didn't say anything in front of my parents, but after I'd finished, he asked if he could speak to me alone.

He told me he loved me, and it was because he loved me so much, he'd divorce me quietly, to avoid shaming me.

I'd known he'd have a hard time believing me—I still couldn't quite believe it myself at times—but I was shocked. Part of me had thought—hoped and prayed—that he'd just marry me sooner, since I wasn't showing yet, in order to give the impression that the baby was a wedding night blessing rather than a pre-wedding accident.

And then, thank God, Joseph had his encounter.

He came to me in tears the next morning, apologizing with more words than I think I'd ever heard escape his lips at once, telling me of the angel and our baby's name.

It was the first time he'd called it "our baby" rather than "your baby."

That would have given me tingles enough if he hadn't gone on to say our baby's name would be Jesus, Yeshua, Immanuel -- "God with us" -- just as the angel had told me.

We were soon married, much to my parents' joy. Although I moved into Joseph's house, and his bed, we did not know each other; we would not until after Jesus' birth.

The birth of the Messiah. Which was coming without trumpets or feasts or resounding orations in the synagogue. Just morning sickness, and afternoon sickness, and evening sickness, and all the aches and pains and weariness that come with pregnancy.

<><><>

I was done being pregnant. It'd been eight long months, and yet I knew I should expect another month before his arrival. Something told me God was going to take His time picking the perfect date.

And place, apparently, because it was then we learned of the census.

Oh, that dreadful census. If it hadn't been for that, I'd have been able to give birth at home amongst family, with support from my mother and sisters.

But no, God had a bigger plan. He had prophecies to fulfill. And one of them meant we had to go to Bethlehem before Jesus could be born.

So we did, me upon a donkey, since there was no way I was going to make it on my aching, swollen feet. Because Joseph was of the line of David, he knew people in town, so he wrote ahead to inquire about a room to stay when we arrived. I was grateful to him, but it was all for naught.

We arrived too late, slowed down by the traffic on the road, the crazy travelers along the way who sped past us with their loaded wagons and fast horses, a steady stream of other people headed to the town of their ancestors to be counted. And me, forced to stop to relieve myself every couple hours, while baby Jesus tried to stretch his legs from within my womb.

By the time we pulled in, Joseph's friend had been unable to hold our room any longer, having so many other visitors with money in their purses to spend on lodging. There was nothing left for a poor young couple just starting out in life with a donkey, a few bags of goods—mostly empty now after the cravings hit on our long journey—and a baby on the way. Thankfully, he looked at my belly, and my tired, sore body barely capable of standing any longer, and took mercy on us. While making apologies, he arranged a sort of bed for us below in the stable with our donkey. We were far from the only inhabitants. There were also horses, cattle, goats that provided the inn's milk, chickens that provided the inn's eggs, and other beasts of provision.

I'll never forget the smell.

I hadn't been able to smell much before I was pregnant, but when I was—and this was true of all my pregnancies—I could smell a rotten egg in Jerusalem.

Part of me still believes the reason I went into labor in that stable was the smell.

It was either empty my stomach or empty my womb and, thankfully, God told my body it was time.

And then, He was there.

<><><>

It all became real in one glorious moment.

The pain was so intense. I knew God must be giving Jesus all the experiences of life He could possibly give from the first to the last. As he slid out of my womb into Joseph's arms, he opened his little mouth and took his first screaming breath.

My entire body relaxed, and I began to cry as Joseph lifted

Jesus into my arms and laid him upon my breast.

There was nothing more to do. He was here.

He was here.

Our God and Savior, our Lord Immanuel, our baby Jesus, was here.

The first time he opened his eyes and looked at me nearly took my breath away.

For one fleeting instant, I was certain I could see all of eternity in his eyes.

I could see Creation, the flood, Abraham, Isaac, all the way to David, and then to Joseph and me.

And then all I could see was myself, my tired, tearful self, reflected in his eyes.

My son. I knew he was God's, but he was also mine.

God had chosen me—*Me*—for a reason. I'll never understand completely why. Why He didn't choose a king's family, or at least a family who was richer, more devout, more ... I don't know ... *something* more than a carpenter and a young girl who were married after He was already on His way.

Why us?

I still don't know. I suppose I never will.

But that's one of the beauties of God. His love and hope fill us up so we don't have to *know* anymore. Because belief is enough. It may not be enough all the time. Sometimes I still doubt He did what He did, and I was there. I saw it. I lived it.

Yet every time I began to doubt, God reminded me it was real.

The shepherds were the first.

There we were, just Joseph and me and a—*finally*—sleeping infant wrapped in swaddling cloths and laid in a manger—much to the curiosity of the donkey, horses, cows, and other creatures—when they appeared.

At first I thought I was dreaming. Their faces were alight with a glow reminiscent of my visit from the angel.

And then I realized, they'd had their own visit.

They apologetically told us angels had appeared to them and told them to come here, directly here, to see the Savior. *Their* Savior.

They didn't tell us much more then because they were overcome and had to kneel, just staring, mesmerized by an infant. There were grown men and boys amongst them, but I knew they'd seen a baby before.

Just not this baby.

And that was when I knew.

Yes, I'd just given birth like other women. Yes, the smell was still a suffocating reminder of where we were currently lying. And yes, these men were not kings or rabbis or perhaps not even Jews, but they'd been chosen to be the first. The first to remind me just what we were about to embark upon.

We were going to raise Jesus, God's Son, to whatever purpose He had chosen.

<><><>

*Thhpppwwwtttt…*

I sighed heavily. As I pulled back the rags, I held my breath.

"Blech!" I cried. "What a sight!"

The baby tucked his bottom lip up under his upper lip and gave me a big-eyed grin.

"You overflowed again?!" I cried.

He cooed softly and reached down to touch—

"Oh, no you don't!"

I swiftly grabbed the chubby little hand and pulled it back just in time.

"Don't touch! It's bad enough without you getting it all over your hands."

He tucked his lip back under and looked at me with large brown eyes.

"Well, all I have to say is you're lucky you're so cute."

He laughed that perfect baby laugh and suddenly all was well again with the world.

I tried not to smile as I pulled out the dirty cloths and threw them in the straw basket beside me, using a damp rag to wipe up what was still sticking to the smooth bottom.

Yuck. Then again, what had I been expecting? That he wouldn't poop and pee like other human beings?

He'd been circumcised, too, like any other baby boy, though unlike others, when we went up to Jerusalem to be purified, I'd never forget that moment when Simeon—one of those men of such righteous and devout faith I could see the glory of the Lord's Spirit about him even as he approached—walked up and cried out, "Here is the One I have been waiting for!"

God had certainly made it clear in those early days that my son was really His Son. I sometimes wondered how Joseph felt about it all, but he'd always been the quiet, brooding sort, much happier with his hands working a piece of wood than standing in a temple orating, or around people in any situation, really.

I reached across my body with my right hand for some clean cloths while holding down pudgy baby hands with my left.

"Why did I put the clean cloths on the left again?" I asked myself.

Baby Jesus gave me a full grin for that one.

"I love you, too," I whispered, squeezing his hands once before tucking the clean cloths under his little bottom and wrapping them securely up and around his middle.

<><><>

The cries were hunger cries. I knew as soon as I heard them, but I was in the middle of washing the large stack of dirty cloths covered in poop and pee and spit-up, and I was up to my thighs in the chilly river water.

On a smooth rock along the riverbed sat the large basket holding my baby, and I called back to him, "I'll be there in just a moment, sweetheart. Just let Mommy finish these cloths."

*WAAAAHHHHH!!!!*

But baby Jesus was having none of it. He was hungry. NOW.

"I'll be there in a moment," I called back again. *Just one more –*

*WAAAAHHHHH!!!!*

Nope. Not going to happen. I grabbed the remaining cloths and threw them on the muddy riverbank as I splashed toward the shore. Who cared if they got dirtier? Certainly not Jesus, as he was the one making this mess.

*WAAAAHHHHH!!!!*

I pulled my skirt down from where I'd tucked it into the rope around my waist to avoid getting it too wet, and hurried to the rock that held the basket.

"I'm coming," I said over the squall, and peeked over the edge. Jesus looked up at me and grinned. No tears. No signs of crying at all. Not even chewing on his hands out of hunger.

He was perfectly fine.

"You're not even hungry!" I shook my head.

Jesus kept smiling at me as I picked him up, the love spilling out of his eyes as he looked at me.

"Did you just want Mommy?" I asked him, and his eyes told me yes.

I held him close and hummed, the wet hem of my skirt slapping my damp ankles as I swayed.

I didn't want to clean those rags anyway.

<><><>

"But, Joseph, you're missing it," I said, as my husband stopped in for a quick bite to eat before heading back out to his workshop.

He worked so long and so hard to support us, but I sometimes wondered if he was using his work as an excuse to stay away. He had willingly accepted the Lord's plan for our family after the angel visited him, but I knew he still doubted.

At least, I did. It was difficult to remember that Jesus was somehow also God made manifest to dwell amongst us when he still nursed at my bosom and thought his own toe the most wonderful thing in all creation.

"I'll be home tonight," Joseph said quietly, giving me a quick kiss on the cheek. He glanced back at Jesus before diving out the door into the darkness.

I sighed and turned to our son, who was using the wall to support himself as he side-stepped along it.

"He does love you," I said with a shrug and a nod that bespoke my conflicted spirit.

"Dada?" Jesus asked, taking one hand off the wall and turning to me.

"Yes. He loves you very much. He just has a lot on his mind."

Even though we'd chosen to stay in Bethlehem, rather than return to Nazareth, the house where we now lived was being paid for by the rough and steady hands of my husband.

My husband, who had listened to God even when it meant stares from everyone in Nazareth, including our own family. I was thankful the census had called us out of Galilee and into Judea—yes, the same census I'd once despised for the same reasons—rather than having to stay any longer amongst those who doubted our tale of God's calling.

Even those who assumed Joseph had married me because Jesus was his own son, come before the completion of our betrothal, would have doubted as he grew.

I could see myself in Jesus' eyes, a little in his nose and chin. But not Joseph. Joseph was not in the curve of his cheeks, or the roundness of his ears. He was not the boy's father, after all.

And yet, when I held Jesus' hands, they seemed to me to have the same courage and strength I found in Joseph's. Something told me they would grow to be carpenter's hands, like his earthly father, and I prayed Joseph might find a connection there that he had yet to feel.

Jesus took another step toward me, his hand still on the wall for balance.

And then, suddenly, he was walking toward me, his hands free of any support, reaching for mine as his legs toddled back and forth across the dirt floor.

But before he could reach me—*bump*! His weight pulled him to the ground again.

My heart filled with joy and pride at his achievement, but once again, Joseph had missed it.

<><><>

His cries woke me first, as they always did, and I carefully slid off our pad without rousing my sleeping husband.

I crept to the corner where Jesus lay, tossing and turning, and crying.

"Shh, shh, shh," I said as I came closer, kneeling down to wipe his sweaty hair from his forehead. "Shh, shh, shh, Mommy's here."

He sat up and threw his arms around my neck.

I held him tightly to me, soaking up his fears into my shoulders, praying softly as I did so.

"When I am afraid, I will trust in you. In God, whose word I praise, in God I trust; I shall not be afraid." It was my favorite scripture, one I'd memorized as a child and stored in my heart. As I prayed to God, holding God, I felt an overwhelming peace, the words comforting and familiar.

"You have kept count of my tossings; put my tears in your bottle. Are they not in your book?" The peace seemed to spread from my heart to Jesus', and I felt his body relax back into the restful attitude of sleep.

"I will render thank offerings to you. For you have delivered my soul from death, yes, my feet from falling, that I may walk before God in the light of life." I gently lay my sleeping son on the mat before me, tucking his blankets about his shoulders, his face still and peaceful now.

I leaned down and kissed his damp forehead firmly, letting my breath and my lips caress the sleeping form of the Son of God, come to dwell with me, in my life, for however long He would allow.

<><><>

I sat down heavily on the dirt floor of the house, small clouds billowing out from beneath my bottom that was still wide enough to tell the world that I'd had a child, even though we'd been married little more than a year.

It was hard to believe it had almost been one year already since the Son of God came to dwell on earth.

And what was he doing?

Picking up dirt clods off the floor and shoveling them into his mouth like they were the best thing he'd ever tasted.

Drool dripped from his teething mouth, turning the dirt into mud on his chin and wet fingers and where it dribbled onto his pudgy little legs.

He leaned forward to grab some more and I shoved a wooden donkey Joseph had whittled for him into his hands, in an attempt to sidetrack him.

He gurgled happily for a minute. It *was* his favorite toy, after all, much to Joseph's delight. But then Jesus tossed it to the side and reached for another dirt clod.

I shook my head and pulled him into my lap. But that only made him wriggle, elbowing me in the belly with a surprisingly pointed joint, given how round the rest of his limbs were.

"Oof!" I breathed, dropping him and rubbing the sore spot. "Fine," I said. "Eat dirt. You made it."

I attempted to stand to leave him to his own devices. Naturally, that was when he decided he needed my attention.

He pulled on my skirts as I rose, looking up at me with a big brown mouth inside and out, a few tears streaking down his cheeks to join the mud.

I bent over to scoop him up and gently kissed him on the only spot still devoid of mud—his forehead.

After all, how much longer would I be able to cuddle the Creator before he was too big to fit in my arms?

<><><>

The wiseman chuckled as he watched Jesus toddle across the floor toward where he knelt, his gift wrapped in the finest silk sitting on the floor before him.

Jesus leaned over, inspecting the package. He seemed to be pondering what it was, as was I.

These wisemen had traveled long and far to see my son. The Son of God. What had they expected? Probably not this dusty house, with a leaking roof that Joseph had yet to fix. Nor a toddler with a runny nose who was currently reaching out with curious little fingers to touch the silk.

Then again, didn't all kings begin this way? Not in a small hovel, and certainly never born and laid to rest where animals gathered to eat. But didn't Herod himself come into this world a mewling infant, taking his first steps slowly and carefully? Even he must have had a runny nose now and then.

Jesus pulled on the ropes around the top of the package so hard it fell over, hitting the ground with a sound that told me whatever was inside wasn't intended to be handled by a child.

"Jesus," I said, my tone of voice making him look at me with the knowledge that he'd done something I'd rather he didn't do.

The wiseman smiled, his eyes never leaving my child. "It is no matter. Here, may I help you?" he asked, reaching forward to set right the package once more.

Jesus nodded and watched as the man's long, brown fingers pulled the rope in such a manner as to loosen the silk in one quick motion, letting it pool at the base of a clay bottle with the most intricate scrollwork I'd ever seen. The potter had created areas of darkness and light, which defined the images of a river lined with reeds, pictures telling a story around the top and bottom.

Jesus tilted his head. He'd never seen a bottle of perfume before, as I could certainly not afford such a thing on Joseph's meager earnings.

Then Jesus reached forward slowly, carefully, and quickly pulled out the silk from beneath the bottle, causing it to crash once again to our floor, though thankfully it was so finely crafted even this did not break it.

"I'm so sorry," I said to the wiseman, but then realized he was laughing, his white teeth flashing between his brown lips.

Jesus held up the silk to him, a smile on his face, as though he knew he'd done something funny—which made me worry he'd do it again.

But then he turned and toddled back to me, dragging the beautiful cloth across the dirt floor as he came.

Then he held it out and I took it.

"Gift," he said with a smile.

And I began to smile, too.

<><><>

Joseph was working late again, so it was just me and Jesus. I cut up his lamb into small pieces, praying that maybe this time he'd eat the meat without complaint.

Like most children I'd known, he hadn't yet "acquired a taste" for meat, but it seemed to me the only thing he had acquired a taste for was bread. Bread for every meal. My hands were growing sore with all the kneading.

"You cannot live on bread alone!" I cried when he refused once again to touch anything else before him.

His lips puckered and his eyes widened, and then he shoved in another fistful of bread.

I shook my head. I decided I was too tired to fight the battle of the lamb tonight. Alone. Again. At least he was growing.

Once we finished, I thought it a warm enough night to attempt a bath. Bathing usually resulted in muddy knees for me and a clean baby Jesus…for about two minutes, until he splashed out of the wooden tub and landed in the mud-soaked earth surrounding it. Nevertheless, I liked to attempt it. There was something akin to pure joy in the happy noises he made while in the water.

I was just pulling the hot water off the fire when Joseph fell through the door.

"Gather your things," he said perfunctorily.

I could see in an instant that something was wrong. My mind raced. Had something happened to one of our families? Were we rushing home to find one of our parents on their deathbed?

"The wisemen had a dream," he said, explaining in his limited-words way as he grabbed cloths, wrapping them around the remains of dinner.

"All of them?" I asked, setting aside the heated water and telling Jesus we were going on a little trip, still unaware of just how far we'd be traveling that night.

"Yes. I had one, too."

I stopped short. "When? Just now?"

"Yes. An angel appeared and told me we must go to Egypt—"

"Egypt?!" I cried.

"Yes."

"For how long?"

Joseph stopped in his rushed packing and turned to me, crossing the small room to take my hands into his. "I don't know," he said, and I realized his hands were shaking. "The wisemen have left. They were warned in a dream that Herod has something terrible planned." His eyes glanced at Jesus, who I'd sent to gather his things—not even two, yet already he was eager to be of help.

My mind flashed to the worst possible idea, that Herod, a king, might have gotten it into his head that my son, the King of Heaven, was here to take his throne. There was only one response a man like Herod would have to that.

Joseph's eyes and short nod of his head told me my thoughts were accurate.

My breath caught in my throat and my heart stopped beating.

This couldn't be God's plan, for His Son to die before he'd even lived two years on this earth. I shook my head. Of course it wasn't. That was why Joseph had been visited by another angel—to protect Jesus, and us, by telling us to run.

"We will go as far as we can tonight. It will be a long journey to the border."

I nodded, gave his rough hands a squeeze, and turned to find Jesus watching us, his head cocked. In his arms and at his feet he'd gathered his gifts from the wisemen—the gold, frankincense, and myrrh, among other things—and I suddenly understood why they'd come at that particular time. They'd given us exactly what was necessary to make this trip possible. We couldn't have afforded it otherwise. Their gifts would provide us with everything we needed to begin a new life.

And once again, I marveled at God's provision, His timing, His perfect plan.

His perfect Son.

I wanted to protect Jesus. I wanted to do everything and anything I could to keep him safe. I knew I would die for him, if that was what God required of me.

Did all mothers feel this way about their child? Especially a firstborn son?

I couldn't ask my mother. I might never speak to her again.

A sudden sadness filled my heart. I might never see any of my family again. We might never return to Judea or Galilee, might never again see the beautiful temple rising on the holy hill of Jerusalem.

But if that was the price God asked of me to keep His Son safe, then I must do it.

It was almost too much.

Getting pregnant before marriage, avoiding the constant stares and murmurings, traveling to Bethlehem in the final month of pregnancy, and then giving birth with no one to help but my husband and a donkey, in a place filled with a stench that was almost unbearable… None of that seemed as difficult as having to leave everyone we loved to go into exile in a country neither of us knew anything about, for as long as the Lord decreed.

<><><>

I sat on the floor of our new home, cradling my sweet firstborn, singing softly to him as he dozed in my arms. I praised God in my singing, thanking Him for delivering us safely out of Herod's hands.

When I had agreed to carry the Lord's child, I hadn't realized there would be so much travel involved. My first time leaving Nazareth had been to see my cousin, and then Joseph and I had traveled up to Bethlehem. And now…now we were refugees. On the run. In exile. In Egypt.

Hadn't God delivered our ancestors from Egypt? Why would He bring us back? And this time with His own Son?

I wondered if it had something to do with a prophecy. Joseph seemed to think almost everything was to fulfill a prophecy, but part of me felt it was just his way of coping without answers.

And yet, as I thought back to that first moment when the angel appeared and told me what was to come…

I sighed. Just thinking about it filled me with that peace again. That restful understanding that God was in control. It was such a relief.

Followed quickly by doubts, anxiety…but then moments of reaffirmation.

I'd doubted and run to Elizabeth, and she'd reaffirmed by telling me about her son John.

I'd doubted and run to Joseph, and he'd reaffirmed by telling me about his own angel encounter.

I'd doubted as I held a squawking new infant in the dirt and grime of a barn, surrounded by the musk of farm animals, and then the shepherds had appeared, and they'd reaffirmed by telling me about the angels who had told them where they must come to find their Savior.

I'd doubted as we tried to raise Jesus to love God as any toddler might be capable of, and then the wisemen had appeared, and they'd reaffirmed by telling me about the star that had led them to worship the new King.

Jesus stirred in my arms and I realized I'd stopped humming. I started again, a song of worship.

It came to my mouth without my even thinking of it. I caressed the round face in my arms as I sang.

"I lift up my eyes to the hills. From where does my help come? My help comes from the Lord, who made heaven and earth. He will not let your foot be moved; he who keeps you will not slumber. Behold, he who keeps Israel will neither slumber nor sleep. The Lord is your keeper; the Lord is your shade on your right hand. The sun shall not strike you by day, nor the moon by night. The Lord will keep you from all evil; he will keep your life. The Lord will keep your going out and your coming in from this time forth and forevermore."

Even as I worshiped my God in my arms, I pondered how our lives had gone so quickly from normal, everyday lives to something out of a scripture story. It filled my heart with dread to wonder if we'd have to travel back to all the places from which God had delivered His children.

Of course, if that was the plan, we'd end up in Eden at the end, and that thought gave me peace. All of it just might be worth it if the end result was Eden. To walk in the garden with God Himself… My heart filled with pure joy to think of it.

I looked down on the sleeping face of baby Jesus.

Then again, if to walk with God was Eden, I was there already.

<><><>

"Well, Mary," Luke asked. "Did you know?"

I shook my head, my eyes dry somehow, even as the memories filled my heart.

"No," I said. I stared at the aged hands that had once held the Messiah. "How could I?"

How could I know he was going to be more than a great rabbi? How could I know he was going to do miracles and mighty wonders? How could I know my son, my baby boy, was going to grow up only to be killed? To be hung on a cross like a criminal, between two criminals? How could I know *that* was God's plan, when all He'd ever asked of me was to deliver His Son? To carry him, raise him, teach him of his Father's love, and then let him go. Just like all mothers were asked to do.

How could I know mine was going to live to die, and then live again, for me?

I'd pondered and wondered and replayed everything over and over, sometimes doubting if it had all really happened. I'd replayed the most holy moments again and again, because in the midst of those normal, everyday events, it was so easy to forget and begin to wonder: How can this little boy be the Son of God?

I couldn't tell Luke everything. I just couldn't.

No one would want to hear a mother's private memories anyway.

They just wanted to hear about the miracles. Of the moments of affirmation that God had blessed us with time and again. Of the angel visits, cousin Elizabeth, the shepherds, Simeon, that moment when he was lost and found again in the temple…all that I could tell. The rest I would keep to myself, like a treasure guarded in my heart.

The better question, I thought, was if I *had* known, would I still have said, "Let it be so," on that ordinary day so long ago when the angel appeared and said I'd give birth to my Savior?

And to that question, I knew immediately the answer was and would always be a resounding *yes*.

– Verses from Psalm 56:3-4 and Psalm 121 (ESV)

# Challah Bread

***Pronounced "hal-lah" this traditional Jewish bread is a soft, enriched bread often made as part of Hanukkah.***

1 T active dry yeast
1 C water
~4 C flour (all-purpose or bread)
2 tsp salt
¼ C honey
2 eggs
1 egg, separated
¼ C vegetable oil

1. Begin by measuring the yeast into a small bowl and pouring the water over it. Make sure the water is warm, but not too hot. Let it sit until a nice froth appears. (If a froth does not appear, your yeast may not be active. Try adding a little honey or sugar to get it going.)
2. In the bowl of a stand mixer with a dough hook, mix together the flour and salt (start with just 4 C of flour).
3. Add the honey, 2 full eggs, 1 egg yolk (save the egg white for later!), oil, and yeast mixture.
4. Mix until combined, then knead the dough with the dough hook on low speed for about 8 minutes. When it's finished, the dough should naturally pull away from the sides of the bowl into a smooth ball, so until it does so, add flour a bit at a time and continue to knead it.
5. Place the dough in an oiled bowl, cover, and place in a warm area to rise until doubled in size, which generally takes about 1-2 hours.
6. Divide the dough into six equal pieces. Roll each piece into 12-15 inch lengths.
7. Now you get to braid the dough! Begin by pinching

together all six ropes on one end and splaying the rest out. Starting with the rope on the far right side, pull it over two ropes, under the third, and over the last two. (That's Over 2, Under 1, Over 2.) Continue to do this, always starting with the rope on the far right side. Weave until you have an entire loaf and squeeze the ends together. Tuck the ends under either end of the loaf so the whole thing is a rounded oval shape.

8. Place the loaf on a baking sheet lined with parchment paper. Dust the loaf with flour, cover, and let it rise again about an hour.
9. Preheat oven to 350°F. Mix the egg white with a little water and gently brush the top of the loaf (don't deflate it!).
10. Bake for 25-35 minutes until brown. Cool and enjoy!

Find Patricia Meredith online:

***www.patricia-meredith.com***
***Facebook, Twitter, & Instagram: @pmeredithauthor***

# Those Who Stayed

***By Ronnell Kay Gibson***

I let the door slam behind me and stomp down the hallway toward the elevator. After I press the down arrow, I shake my wrists, hoping to shed some of the anger and fear off my tightened muscles. But it doesn't help.

Waiting for the door to open, the familiar Christmas tune of "peace on earth and good will toward men" mocks me. I can't wait any longer. I abandon the elevator and just start wandering. Past the hospital rooms, past the nurses' station, past the little lobby with relatives waiting for news.

Rage begins to build. My heart beats faster. My chest feels like a caged animal ready to explode at any moment.

I see a room marked, "Chapel."

I duck inside to get a respite. But instead, my hardened facade ruptures, sending emotions crashing in, overwhelming me. With them come the memories of a Christmas Eve twenty years ago.

Just like then, I am powerless to move.

<><><>

I had exhausted all other ideas.

It was our last Christmas with Grandma Gen, or at least at Grandma Gen's house. The following week, her house was to be sold, and she'd be moving into a nursing home.

My quest was to find something special for her. Not just regular special, extraordinarily special.

Tonight was Christmas Eve. Dinner would be served in less than an hour, and I couldn't show up empty-handed.

Jesus' Little Lambs bookstore was my last resort.

When I stepped out of the car, my foot sank into an inch of snow, and the arctic wind tried to tear through my clothes. I zipped up my jacket.

On the sidewalk, I quickened my pace and rushed in front of a mom with a small boy. I grabbed and held open the store's front door handle for them.

The woman's voice echoed a hint of surprise. "Thank you, young man."

Her son looked up at me, his red Elmo cap almost covering his eyes. His wide grin showed off a missing front tooth. "What's your name?"

"I'm Henry. What's yours?"

"Elmo."

"Nice to meet you, Elmo."

The bells clanked on the glass as the door shut behind us. Warmth enveloped me. I stomped the excess snow off my boots and shook the flakes out of my short, brown curls.

I'd never been in the bookstore before. I expected a dark, dank place with statues of the Virgin Mary everywhere, but this store was filled with bright fluorescent lights, festive decorations, and jolly Christmas music. As the smell of cinnamon and evergreen greeted me, my body relaxed.

Somewhere in the countless rows of books and trinkety stuff, I knew I could find something. The perfect gift to hide the fact that nothing would be the same after this Christmas. No more rolling cut-out cookies at Grandma's kitchen island, laughing as we got flour up our noses. No more Christmas Eve dinners piled with enough food for many, but seating for just us three. No more mornings settled in front of the artificial tree, sparkling with white and blue lights, listening as she read Dad and me the Christmas story.

I worked my way up and down the aisles and through the crowd of last-minute shoppers, scanning each shelf for gift inspiration.

Behind a middle-aged man with a bowler hat, a twinkle light caught my eye. I waited till he moved aside and stepped in to take a closer look. On the shelf sat a crystal angel holding a red jeweled heart. As I picked it up, light reflected in every direction.

This was it.

My first paycheck as a busboy wasn't much, but I wanted to use it to buy her something nice for her new place. I held my breath as I checked the price. Yes. My wallet held enough cash for that and maybe a candy-cane latte from the coffee shop next door. Sweet.

I headed toward the cash register. I was so jazzed about my find, I didn't even care I had to get in a long line of restless customers.

When the bells on the front door sounded, an icy chill shot through my heart.

I turned around. My nerves froze.

A man with a long camo jacket stood, feet set apart, in the doorway. A semiautomatic rifle was poised in his hands. His unzipped coat revealed a wrinkled, black T-shirt. Deep purple circles were embedded underneath crazed eyes. His face was rough, pale, and unshaven.

The warmth drained from my face, replaced by frigid fear.

Firing a couple rounds into the ceiling, he shouted, "Nobody move!" Then charged in.

Screams erupted. People crouched to the floor, covering their heads. Elmo and his mom ducked behind a Veggie Tales display.

Those in line with me ducked to the ground, but I couldn't move. With my back up against the check-out counter, I just stood stunned, clutching the angel ornament to my heart.

The gunman fired again, this time at music posters high on the back wall. "Everyone, shut up!"

The cries ceased. The only sound was the chorus of "Silent Night" over the loudspeaker.

"And someone shut that crap off."

The lady behind the counter made a slow and deliberate turn, her hands shaking as she pressed some sort of button. The music stopped mid "holy."

As the gunman stepped forward, tan work boots left behind snowy footprints. He mumbled something about the absurdity of that song.

Every muscle tensed as he moved toward me. My nose scrunched at the stench of alcohol and body odor. He stopped a few feet away.

The gunman's deep voice bellowed through the store. "Some of you are going to die today."

Some of the hostages let out muffled cries.

Hostages. That's what we had become.

Paralyzing fear surged through my veins.

The gunman's voice was deep and steady. "I'll let some of you go. It's your choice."

I held my breath, awaiting his demands. Money? Revenge?

World peace?

"Since you're in this so-called *Christian* bookstore, you must think you're a Christian." The gunman paced through the crowd, towering above the crouched people, leveling his rifle at their heads.

"But what do you truly believe? Here it is: If you can say you do NOT believe Jesus was the son of God, you can leave. I'll let you go." He waved his free arm in mock surrender. "Those foolish enough to believe are delusional. Either way, decide carefully because those who stay will be shot."

In horrifying silence, the offer hung in the air.

I digested his offer. Could I really just go? I had no beef with the man from Nazareth, but I had no allegiance to Him, either.

Unlike the erratic beating of my heart, the antique clock behind me clicked in perfect rhythm. The only sound.

Tick.

Tick.

Tick.

This was the kind of thing you read about in the papers, not something that could happen in our small town, Fond du Lac, Wisconsin.

I ordered my feet to move, but they rebelled, frozen in place. My whole body was. Maybe it knew this was just a trick.

"So, what's it gonna be?" The guy spun around, probably looking for any sign of movement.

There was none.

"Don't believe me? Here." He clicked on the safety latch and hung the long black strap over his shoulder.

Still, no one moved.

Three trembling breaths.

Four.

Five.

A stirring to my right. A man in a tailored, black trench coat rose. He clutched a black briefcase and dashed toward the front door.

I stared at the gunman to see what he'd do.

He did nothing but watch.

As the businessman exited, his briefcase got caught in the door. He gave one good yank, and it came loose, sending him tumbling backward onto the sidewalk.

The gunman laughed, sounding like a shopping mall Santa. "We have our first denial. Anyone else ready to choose their life over their God?"

He hoisted himself onto the counter a few feet away and sat, the gun cradled in his lap. The woman behind the register stepped back, her eyes darting from him to the front door. Trembling, she stretched her bony arm out for something under the ledge he rested on, careful not to get any closer than necessary. Grabbing her purse, she clutched it to her chest, letting the long leather strap dangle. After sidestepping her way around the counter, she fled.

One by one, people began to rise. Those next to me in line, those from unseen places of the store. Our captor grinned, teeth beaming like the Cheshire cat's. He nodded as each person passed by. Did he want everyone to leave? Did he really NOT want to kill any of us? What was the point to all of this?

Elmo and his mother stepped out from behind a cardboard cut-out of Bob the Tomato. She grasped the arm of a well-dressed woman who had gathered up her large shopping bag, ready to leave.

"Please, take my son Matthew." As she spoke, she handed the lady something. "This is my husband's business card. Please call him. Tell him I love him. Tell him...I had no choice."

The woman looked down at the boy, then glanced over her shoulder at the gunman. He stared at them, his head tilted to the side, his eyebrows raised.

"Okay," the woman with the shopping bag whispered. "I promise."

The mother knelt so she was eye-to-eye with her son. "Matty, go with this nice lady. Later on, Daddy will come get you. Always, always, remember I love you."

Matthew scrunched his eyes and shook his head. "Mommy, the bad man said to leave if we don't believe in Jesus. But I *do* believe in Jesus. I can't lie. I need to stay and stand up for Jesus, too."

Tears fell from his mother's eyes. I expected her to argue with him, but she bit her lower lip then nodded. "You're right, Matty. Jesus came into your heart, just like He did mine. We promised we would live for Him forever...no matter what." As she got back on her feet, the boy swung his mother's hand with one hand and took off his Elmo hat with the other. He smiled up at her.

The lady with the shopping bag shook her head in dismay or maybe disgust. As she hurried out the front door, the business card fell from her fingers and floated to the floor.

*Hey, come back,* I wanted to shout.

How would she find Matthew's dad? How would he know how painful this decision was for his wife? Or how it was his son's choice to stay?

*I'll do it. I'll grab the business card. I'll tell the story.*

But my body was still in lockdown. I couldn't wiggle my toes, squeeze my abs, or feel the weight of the glass angel in my hand.

*I'm sorry, Elmo.*

An elderly gentleman with a wooden cane hobbled up behind me. As he passed, I sniffed a pungent combination of Ben-Gay and Old Spice. A plaid cap covered his head, with just a few gray hairs sticking out from underneath. His airman's jacket was zipped up to his chin.

He made his way over to Elmo and his mom and put a hand on her shoulder. She straightened her back, took a deep breath, and wiped her tears.

A young couple I hadn't noticed before appeared from the back. As they walked toward the three standing together, I noticed a large bulge protruding from underneath the girl's ski jacket. Was she pregnant? They looked about my age. The girl gave the mother a tearful hug, then stood on the other side of her.

At the sight of them, the gunman spat to the side.

His apparent disgust churned my stomach. These were people's lives, their futures, he planned to cut short. Now I was the one who wanted to spit a big ol' loogie.

In the front of the store stood an older lady. A white waitress uniform peeked out from underneath her ruby-red, fuzzy coat. Her thinning blond hair was wound into a loose bun, held in place with silver clips. From her location, it'd be only three steps to the store's exit. Instead, she left the doorway, and the people who were still filing out, behind. Her red-and-green jingle bell earrings announced her determined approach. She positioned herself next to the old man.

The gunman sat atop his perch, smiling at people as they

headed out of the store. No one met his stare. No one looked back.

I didn't blame them. I would've left, if I could've. Then the gunman would've smiled at me too.

One final couple walked toward the group, coming from the rear of the store. Probably in their forties, both wore expensive-looking wool coats and fancy shoes. Their arms were wound around each other as they trod forward.

I recognized the man. He was the pastor of the largest church in town. I'd visited there once with Grandma Gen. That Sunday, he'd spoken fiercely about the love of God and the punishment for sins. I'd been impressed. But not impressed enough to go back.

Of course they were coming to take a stand for Jesus with the others. As the pastor approached the huddled group, a lone tear ran down his cheek. However, he and his wife didn't stop. They kept walking. His eyes were glued to the floor.

The wife rubbed her husband's shoulder with her manicured fingers. As they passed me, she whispered to him, "This is not what God has planned for your life. You have so much more to do for Him. Your church needs you. Your family needs you."

They exited the store, stepping into the cold late-afternoon light. Through the window, I saw him look back briefly before he got into his car and drove away.

He left us. How could he have abandoned us like that? It didn't make sense. If the *pastor* left, why did the others stay?

Why was *I* staying? I had no desire to become a religious martyr.

*Please, run.* Again, my feet refused to obey what I told them.

*Please, please, please.*

I remained because, like a deer caught in headlights, I could not move.

I resigned myself to my fate.

Of the many shoppers, only seven of us were left. Six of them stood together. I stood alone.

"That's so much better." The gunman jumped off the counter and headed for the front door. He twisted the dead bolt. As it clicked in place, the sound echoed inside my ears.

"Don't you just hate those so-called *Christians*?" He waved his empty hand toward the exit and strode back to us. "They say they love God, but it's just a scam. They want religious brownie points, trying to earn enough to get to a fictional heaven." He continued with his tirade, pacing back and forth, his voice mocking. "*'I'll pray for you.' 'God has a master plan.'* All of it is foolishness. What good is prayer? What do they know about God? They stand on top of their religious soapboxes, looking down their noses at the rest of us sinners. It's just an act. Look to Jesus on Sunday mornings, look out for yourselves the rest of the week."

He leaned his back against the end of the counter and slid down to the floor. Legs up to his chest, he put his forehead against his knees, gun pointed up, one hand still on the trigger. "Just once, I want someone to tell me the truth." His voice cracked. "I want them to admit they *don't* have all the answers. They *don't* understand what God is doing. That it's okay to be hurt and angry."

Staring at this broken man huddled on the floor, compassion swelled, creating a confusing swirling in my brain. *I* too wanted the truth. *Is there a God? If there is, why do so many bad things happen to good people?* Good people like my mom. She used to take us to church when I was little. I was three when a drunk driver killed her. My dad hadn't set foot in a church since.

The old man with the wooden cane broke the silence. His voice held a hint of a southern drawl. "Seems to me, son, that life's been rough on you. Maybe you came here searchin' for answers."

The gunman leapt up, his face flushed, eyes red, and voice bitter. "The only answer I'm searching for is this." He lunged at the old man. The others took a step backward. He pointed the rifle at the side of the man's skull, knocking his plaid cap to the floor. "Are you ready to die for your Jesus?"

*Just say no,* I tried to telepathically tell the old man. *It's just a word.* I said it all the time.

He slowly turned his head until the barrel of the rifle pointed between his eyes. His posture was straight, his face showed no fear. "From the first moment He revealed Himself to me, I was ready to die for my Savior. But, son, Jesus is asking *you* if you're ready to *live* for Him."

"Don't push me, old man! I have your life in my hands!"

"Son, you may have a gun to my head, but my life's in the hands o' the Lord. You can't do anything that God hasn't already planned for me. If I die today, it'll be a joy to see Him in Heaven. If not, I'll suffer in this old, decaying body, lovin' and servin' Him faithfully."

"You keep believing that, mister. We'll see when a bullet goes through your brain."

I tightened my muscles, bracing myself for a gunshot I was sure would come. It didn't. Instead, the gunman removed the rifle from the man's face, shaking his head and muttering curse words under his breath.

My shoulders relaxed, though the ice in my blood gave me a chilly shudder. I couldn't believe the gunman didn't do…anything.

"And you…" He erected himself in front of Elmo and his mom. She pulled Elmo closer to her.

I tensed as the gunman pointed his rifle at her, then at Elmo's head.

"Are you ready to sacrifice your son to your God?"

Neither of the two flinched. Maintaining unbelievable control, the mom stared at the man. "Matthew is *His* child. I'm just the lucky one who gets to raise him to know our Savior."

"What's that supposed to mean, lady?"

"After nine long years, God answered our prayers for a child. We named him Matthew because it means 'gift of God.' Since then, Matty has had three major surgeries in six years. Each time, the doctors weren't sure he'd make it." The mother swipes at a stray tear. "I've faced losing him so many times, but his life has always been in the hands of the Lord."

I wanted to hear more, but the gunman wasn't interested in her emotional story. Using the barrel of the rifle as a crutch, he squatted down to look in the eyes of the blond-haired boy.

In a calm voice, he asked, "Matthew, do you understand that you could die here today? Do you understand what it means to die?"

Elmo glanced up at his mother as if asking permission to answer.

She squeezed his hand. "It's okay, Matty."

He looked back at the gunman. "When you die you get to go to Heaven to live with Jesus forever. Well, the people who love Jesus will. The ones who don't are going…" He pointed to the floor and whispered, "Down there. To hell."

I held my breath.

But the gunman didn't react cruelly to the child's innocent

words. He just stood up and patted the boy on the head. "Cute kid."

*Whew.*

Then he turned to the young couple. "You two. You're married?"

The young woman cowered behind her husband. He nodded.

"How old are you?"

"I'm nineteen. My wife's eighteen."

"Got your whole life ahead of you. And, by the looks of her, a family, too. Can you really stand here and say you're ready to die?"

The father-to-be looked down. He opened his mouth, but no words came out.

The gunman waited.

The young man cleared his throat. "I'm not ready to die. I'm just starting to live my life."

"Then why stay?"

The young man swallowed. "Well, I've got to do the right thing."

"I would think doing the right thing would be taking care of your family."

"I used to be really good at taking care of myself. I thought I controlled my own destiny. Then Carly got pregnant, and I thought my future was over. I was confused and desperate. Then I realized my only hope was to surrender my life to God. When I did that, He gave me a new set of dreams, ones that included a wife and a child with Jesus as the head of our family."

His wife spoke for the first time, her eyes full of tears. "I want to live." She rubbed her stomach. Her voice was so quiet, I strained to hear. "I want my baby to live, but I can't deny Jesus or what He's done for me…for us."

I thought of all the teenage parents. How many of them actually got married, promised to faithfully love each other and their baby? Not many. And here was a young couple doing just that, and now this? It wasn't fair.

None of it was.

Where was God in all this?

Sirens blared outside, cutting through the silence and the young wife's tender words. Several sets of red and blue lights screeched to a halt in front of the store. A crowd of blue uniforms arranged themselves in tactical positions.

A surge of hope electrified my body. We were still trapped, but we weren't alone. Help had arrived.

But when the gunman shrugged, his lack of concern worried me. And the fact that he wasn't wearing a mask. There was no good end to this situation.

With casual indifference, he lifted his rifle and shot a few rounds into the ceiling. The officers ducked behind their vehicles.

The gunman returned to his interrogation. "What about you, lady? You gonna tell me some weepy story about how God answered your prayers? How He's always the hero swooping in to make everything better?"

"He is my hero." The waitress's voice quivered. "But He didn't answer my prayers, at least not the way I wanted."

His eyebrows scrunched down, his lips pulled to the side.

The waitress took a deep breath. "My husband and I were married for three years when he was in an accident on the construction site. He was rushed to the hospital with severe head trauma. I prayed constantly. Our church and our friends prayed, too. After two weeks, the doctors said his vitals were finally improving. We were so thankful God had heard our prayers. I believed the worse was over, but later that night, he died."

The ache in my heart was a screwdriver twisting my insides raw. I knew that pain. I was little, but I still remembered. Every day, I remembered.

Up to now, nothing the others had said got much of a reaction from him, but now the gunman stared right at her, captivated.

"I wasn't even there when he died." As she continued, her voice grew louder, more passionate. "I was devastated…and angry. Angry at his company. Angry at the doctors. Angry at every person who told me, 'he's in a better place.' How could they say that? His place was with me!" She poked her chest with a stiff finger. "I got *really* angry at God. How could He let this happen? I served Him faithfully my whole life. Read my Bible, prayed, went to church. How could He steal my husband from me?"

Like my mom was stolen from me.

The ice in my veins started thawing, creating an avalanche of emotions.

The guy cocked his head to the side. "Yet you stand here today, ready to die for the God who robbed him from you?"

His interruption brought the woman back to the present. Her voice returned to a kind, motherly tone. "Because even during my darkest anguish, the blackest time of my life, I could not deny that Jesus is still God, and that He still loves me.

"Many don't understand, God doesn't cause us pain. It's because of the sin in this world that there's sickness, sadness, and death. God doesn't harm us. He's waiting to comfort us, to give us peace, to give us joy in the midst of our heartache."

"How? How can you feel joy when you're in such pain?" His voice was raw, pleading for help.

My eyes pooled. *Yes, how?*

She took a step closer and touched his arm—the one that held the gun.

My stomach fluttered.

They stared at each other.

"Because of who He is. Our Creator. Our Savior. He brings peace when there's no peace. He brings hope when there's no hope."

The reverence of the moment was shattered when an officer's voice boomed through the bullhorn outside. "We have you surrounded. You have one minute to release the hostages and come out with your hands up."

For the first time since walking into the store, the gunman looked like he didn't know what to do or say. Then he did what I'd been dreading this entire time.

He turned to me.

I had no choice. I looked directly at him. He sized me up, staring into my eyes, then straight into my soul. He saw my hollow heart. I knew it the instant he turned away from me. Unlike the others, I had nothing to offer him. No miracle, no story of faith, no personal experience with Jesus.

The waitress continued, "You came here today because you wanted to hear the truth. The truth is that, in this world, we all have times of sorrow and doubt. But God is by our side in the midst of each of those trials, pouring out His peace, joy, and love."

He shook his head. "I'm not like you. I don't believe."

The man with the cane stepped forward. "Yes, you do, son. You could've come in here and killed everyone in sight, but you didn't. You pointed your rifle at each one of us, but you didn't pull the trigger. Jesus has been calling you. You just couldn't hear Him through all your anger and grief."

As the old man spoke, heat raced through me. My palms became hot and clammy. The angel ornament I held for my grandma dropped from my hands and shattered on the floor.

The gunman swiveled at the crashing sound, his gun following.

I heard a loud *pop*.

I squeezed my eyes shut. *This is it. We're going to die.*

*I'm sorry, Grandma, I never got to tell say thank you. For who you are and all you've done for me.*

But when I opened my eyes, it was the gunman whose eyes were wide with surprise.

Outside, one of the officers stood behind a vehicle, his arms extended, gun in hand, pointed into the store.

*Pop.*

The gunman fell back.

The hostages crouched down once again. But this time around the wounded man. All but me. My back remained up against the counter.

As the gunman lay on his back, the two small holes in his black shirt began to ooze.

The waitress pulled off her white scarf and pressed it against the wounds, instantly soaking it red. "It's okay. It'll be okay," she cooed.

The man tried to speak. He choked and coughed, spitting up blood.

Out front, a bullhorn sounded. "Release the hostages and come out with your hands up."

The pregnant woman got up on her knees and propped the man's head up onto what was left of her lap. He reached up his hand, and Elmo's mother grabbed and squeezed it.

His lips, stained in blood, moved a little. Finally, he found his voice. He peered up at the women. "Forgive me?"

All three nodded.

"Can Jesus forgive me?"

The older woman nodded tearfully. "It's why we celebrate Christmas, a baby born to save us from our sins. He's waiting. All you have to do is ask."

He dipped his head, tears leaking from the corner of his eyes.

Everyone, except me, bowed their head as she began to pray. "Dear Lord Jesus, we thank You that You are our Maker. We pray for this young man who has struggled to experience Your love. He admits he is a sinner and that he needs a Savior. Forgive him of his sins. Help him to turn from his old life. Make him a new creation through Your love."

The gunman moved his lips in agreement.

When the waitress paused, the old man took over. "We thank You, Lord, that You have saved this young man's soul. Now, we pray You'll save his body. Please keep him with us so that he may experience the joy of livin' for You."

There was a small chorus of "amens." The last and loudest came from the man lying on the ground. His skin was ashen, and his blood had saturated the waitress's scarf, turning it the same color as her coat.

But it wasn't the blood that held my attention. It was his expression. Before, his eyes had been dark and cold, his mouth in a permanent scowl, full of hate and bitterness. Though his physical life was draining from him, his eyes were now bright and alive. His tears were honest, his smile blissful. I couldn't explain it, but I knew I had just witnessed a genuine transformation.

As he lay in the arms of the pregnant woman, the man strained to lift his head. He looked directly at me. "Kid," he whispered. "Let go of the pain. God's waiting for you, too." Then he closed his eyes, and his body went limp.

The SWAT team barreled in behind me.

<><><>

The seven of us who stayed behind that day became instant celebrities, labeled as heroes by the media. I didn't feel like a hero. I felt like a coward. The others tried to tell the whole story, but the most important element, the part about forgiveness and rebirth, was glossed over by reporters.

Four days after the incident, sitting at the breakfast table, I picked up the newspaper lying there. On the front cover were seven small photographs—a snapshot of each of us hostages. Above those was a slightly larger photo of an eighth person. Although I knew it must be the gunman, he didn't look like the man we encountered. In the photo, he was clean-shaven. His hair was trimmed, and he was smiling. He wore a dark suit and striped tie. Beneath the picture was his name: Jonathon Logan Haverson.

I skipped the reporter's embellished account of what happened inside the bookstore and found his biography.

A week before Jonathon Haverson walked into Jesus' Little Lambs bookstore, he was fired from his job at the local paper factory when he showed up at work intoxicated. His boss reported that, up until that time, Jonathon had a spotless record. Speculations formed that his drinking began six months before when he and his family were in a car crash. His wife and two young children were killed instantly.

That was why he could relate to the waitress's story. It was similar to his own. And to mine.

As I folded the paper and pushed it aside, I tried to tuck the entire episode away with it.

But I still couldn't sleep. Every time I closed my eyes, all I saw was the gun, the tears of the man who held it, the way he'd seen right through my façade. His last words haunted me. "Let go of the pain. God's waiting for you too."

I had always thought of myself as a Christian. Though I rarely went to church, I believed there was a man named Jesus, only I hadn't had any need for Him. Looking back now, I knew I was meant to be in the store that day. I should have been the first one out the door, but from the moment Haverson fired his first shot, I was powerless to move.

<><><>

It's been twenty years since that day in the bookstore and ever since, I've tried to ignore what happened. Tried to ignore the fear that paralyzed me. Tried to ignore what the gunman said as he breathed his last breath. I've refused to let myself feel any stirring emotions, to embrace any lessons taught.

Three months ago, I found out my nine-year-old daughter has stage four cancer. Today, on Christmas Eve, the doctors tell me she probably won't live through the night. I have experienced the denial, the resentment. I have yelled and cried and blamed everyone around me, including God.

I have become Jonathon Haverson, desperate for answers.

While my wife sits with our daughter, I slide into a pew in the hospital's chapel. I ignore the Christmas lights and the tree full of handmade ornaments that patients have created.

After all this time, I allow the events of that day to come rushing back, flooding my heart and mind. The words that were said to the gunman, are now meant for me.

For the first time, I believe God had me in the bookstore for a reason. More importantly, I finally understand why.

Once more, I'm rooted to the floor.

This time, I'm on my knees.

## The background to *Those Who Stayed*

Ronnell was inspired to write *Those Who Stayed* after a dream she had where a man with a gun walked into her local Christian bookstore and shouted the same words as the gunman in the story. And in the dream, *she* was the main character, feet cemented to floor, unable to speak or move. When she awoke, the "what ifs" swirled around in her creative brain until she had the story, the characters, and the dialogue. Tying it all together was a bit harder until family friends went through their own tragedy of loss. It was important to her to include what drove the gunman to his desperate act, his redemption, but also the impact of that day on that seventeen-year-old boy years later. In essence, the story coming full-circle. Her hope is that readers will realize that we don't always understand why bad things happen, but we can know with full assurance that God is *always* good.

## Candy Cane Latte recipe

Ingredients:

Instant espresso powder or coffee beans for two shots (2 oz.) espresso

6 oz. milk (or favorite milk substitute)

Peppermint syrup

Crushed candy cane pieces

Whipped cream and chocolate syrup(optional)

1. Add three pumps of peppermint syrup or 1 tablespoon to an 8 oz mug.
2. Brew your coffee as you would for two ounces of coffee using an espresso or dark roast, or you can use instant espresso mix. Add to the mug.
3. Warm your milk either in the microwave (about 40

seconds, careful not to scorch, between 140-180 degrees if using a food thermometer) or on the stovetop. Pour it over the coffee.

4. Froth the latte with a milk frother. There are many different types and prices, but for a beginner, the cheaper frothers work just as well. Some of the more expensive kinds will warm the milk as it froths, saving you a step.

5. Add a dollop of whipped cream and a drizzling of chocolate syrup (optional)

6. Sprinkle crushed candy canes on top. Some stores sell crushed candy cane pieces, or simply put a candy cane in a sealed sandwich baggie and pound with a rolling pin or heavy object.

Enjoy!

<><><>

Find Ronnell Kay Gibson online:

***Youth Leader & YA Writer***
***www.nowdontfreakout.com***
***Facebook: Ronnell Kay Gibson, YA Writer***
***Twitter: @RonnellKay***
***Instagram: ronnellgibson***

## A Rose from the Ashes

### *by JPC Allen*

Glancing left and right, I crunched across the frozen weeds to the abandoned children's home. I could not afford to be spotted now. If only I could take a few seconds and snap some pictures. The light from the early December sunset was perfect. Gashes of blood-red light seeped through the clotted clouds, creating an ominous background for the gray stone building that was rumored to be the scene of a murder.

At the back wall of the home, I slung the strap for my camera across my chest and climbed through an opening that once held a window. I dropped to the bare ground, my long, dark gold braid catching on a loose nail in the sill. I disentangled myself and crossed the dirt floor. The fire had burned the wooden floor away. And the roof and the whole interior. The four stone walls loomed above me like a medieval fortress as the sunset's rays spotlighted sections of the garbage-strewn floor.

I knelt by a large fireplace, straining to detect any sound of psychics, ghost hunters, or thrill-seeking high school kids who had come to catch sight of the ghost of Bella Rydell.

Nothing but a few caws from crows and sighs as the wind sailed through the empty window frames.

A lonely place. Very lonely, stuck on twenty acres of unused county land.

Shaking off a shiver, I unzipped my down vest and removed the two roses. I laid them on the rusty iron grate of the fireplace.

These would start everyone in the county talking again.

I retraced my path to the window opening, hoisted myself onto the sill, then sat suspended, my right leg swaying.

What was that?

Scrutinizing the naked trees, black against the dimming sun, I held my breath.

Wind. Just wind, rattling the dried-up weeds. No people.

Exhaling, I landed on the brittle grass and ran into the woods.

As I approached my battered, black truck, I took a few pictures. If someone saw me, I could say, with halfway honesty, I was out here capturing the sunset.

An hour later, in my one-room apartment over Mrs. Blaney's garage, I warmed my hands around a mug of tea and stared at three wrinkled envelopes.

Jason Carlisle. Walter R. Malinowski IV. Terence O'Neil.

Those names on the envelopes were burned into my brain.

I set down my mug, picked up my phone, and scrolled through photos until I found my favorite. My mom and I stood on a beach in North Carolina. She was in front since she didn't even come to my shoulder. Her brown hair had grown back long enough to mousse and brush back, and her cheeks had filled out so the bones didn't look razor sharp. I touched her beaming smile.

*Mom, I'll do what you want. I promised. But I've got to do it my own way.*

Since I'd placed the first pair of roses in the grate on Halloween night, I'd gotten to know the men attached to the names a little better.

But I still didn't know which one was my father.

Or which one tried to murder my mother twenty years ago.

Or if my father and her attacker were one and the same.

<><><>

"Is this yours, Rae?" My boss, Barb Hanson, held up a phone. "Or did someone leave it here last night?"

"No, ma'am." I straightened from where I was digging into the bin under the drop box. "It's mine."

Barb glanced at it. "You were looking up the Ohio Revised Code?" Her eyebrows lifted above her bright red glasses. "When I was nineteen, the closest I got to reading the law was legal thrillers."

"Yes, ma'am." I rolled the hem of my sweater. "Someone mentioned statute of limitations to me, and I wondered exactly what that meant."

Moving over to a computer on the counter, Barb smiled. "You're curious. That's a good quality for a librarian."

"I'm just a check-out clerk."

"Many librarians start out as check-out clerks."

Hooking my hair behind my ears, I returned to the bin and

loaded items onto a book cart. Bright morning light streamed through the two-story windows, warming the creamy plaster, giving the library lobby the appearance of a home instead of an old row building on Main Street.

Papers rustled behind me, and Barb said, "Mal's going to skewer whoever is trespassing at the children's home...as soon as he can catch them."

Over my shoulder, I glimpsed Barb holding the latest edition of *The Marlin County Recorder*. "What does it say?"

"The sheriff found another pair of roses in the fireplace there. And they weren't there yesterday."

"I know Marlin County is pretty small," I placed a DVD case on the cart, "but the paper gives those roses a lot of space."

"Rick runs the articles as a public service, Rae. Each time Mal has confirmed that someone's left roses, Rick prints a story about how unsafe that old building is." She snorted. "It wasn't safe even before the fire, and that was twenty years ago."

I pushed the cart over to the counter, and Barb and I began checking items in with the scanners.

Aiming for a casual tone as I brushed back runaway strands, I said, "So do you think Bella Rydell died in the fire? You knew her, didn't you?"

"I knew *of* her." Barb's thin lips pressed together tightly. "I was barely in high school when Bella held sway over the male population of the county. I knew enough to avoid her when she showed up at parties held at the home." She shook her head. "I don't know what my sister was thinking, dragging me along with her friends to those parties. I never felt safe there. That place was a tragedy waiting to happen."

I rehooked my hair. Maybe I should have braided it. It looks best hanging loose since it's thick and burns gold when the light catches it at the right angle. But this morning, I could barely tame it, and now it seemed determined to annoy me. "So if Bella did die there, the fire could have been an accident."

"One stray cigarette could have started it." Barb laid aside a book but didn't reach for another. "But no, I don't think Bella died in the fire. No human remains, or any remains, were found. It takes an extremely hot fire to destroy bones. I learned that years ago researching a patron's question about it." She fingered her chin.

"The woman who asked had a horse's hind end for a husband. I've always wondered if she was doing research for practical application."

The time on the screen read 9:02. "Do you want me to open the doors?"

"Yes and set out the newspapers on the table. I'll finish here."

With the keys jangling in my hand and the newspapers under my arm, I crossed to the glass front doors.

Since it was Tuesday, Professor Terence O'Neil was waiting outside in the brilliant sunshine.

"Good morning, sir." I held the door open.

The man darted inside, puffing clouds, stamping his feet. "How many times do I have to tell you, Rae? Call me Terry."

I smiled like a tooth hurt. Having been raised in the South, I couldn't get used to calling my elders by their first names, which seemed to be the usual practice in Ohio.

Pulling off his leather gloves, Terry grinned up at me. "Did you get a chance to watch *Double Indemnity*?"

"Yes." I'd even made a list of things I had noticed so I'd have something to talk about with him. "I didn't expect the ending at all."

"It's one of the best." He slapped snow off his cap.

Terence O'Neil was my idea of a professor. Over sixty, balding, with a closely cut black and white beard covering cheeks that shook when he talked. He even smoked a pipe.

"If you like film noir, Rae, you should try *The Maltese Falcon* or *The Asphalt Jungle.*" Terry had a mellow voice that must have been easy to listen to in class. Or fall asleep to.

"I've heard of *The Maltese Falcon.*" I placed the newspapers on the table between two chairs, then walked around the check-out desk to the computer.

He dropped his books in front of me with a thump. "I should hope so. Even someone as young as you are should know an American classic." He rested his elbows on the counter. "What was your favorite part?"

I tugged at my ear lobe. I didn't have a favorite part. Not because the movie was so old. I'd watched old musicals with my mom. I just didn't like this movie. "I noticed the lighting and how you said it set the mood. It's really different from a color movie."

Leaning closer, he said, "That's your photographer's instinct. Film noir wouldn't be what it is without low-key lighting." He launched into a description of the technique while I checked his books in, removed old program flyers from their plastic holders, and slipped in new ones.

When he paused for a breath, I said. "Did you see the latest article on the mysterious roses?"

Terry scowled the same way he did any time I had brought up the roses. "I don't read speculative trash. Rick Carlisle should know better than to print such garbage."

"Barb thinks he does it as a favor to Sheriff Malinowski, to let people know if they go out there, they could be charged with trespassing."

"The kids who would do that don't read the paper."

"But their parents do." Tilting my head to one side, I said, "It's strange, the roses appearing after so many years. From what I've heard, someone placed a single rose in the grate each year for five years. Then it stopped. Now the roses are back, and there are two of them."

"Really, Rae." He pushed off the desk. "You are an intelligent girl. You shouldn't read anything into—"

"Terence!" Mrs. O'Neil, the professor's wife and member of the library board, stood in the open door of the library, unleashing a blast of cold air that might not have come from outside. "We need to leave."

The professor's shoulders slumped. "Yes, Melissa." He turned to his wife as she marched toward him.

As old as her husband and skeleton-skinny, Mrs. O'Neil had short, white hair that was as icy as her personality. "You haven't anything to check out, Terence?"

"No." He rubbed his beard.

"You spent all your time chattering away with Miss Riley." She aimed deeply sunken eyes my way. "If he is keeping you from your duties, you should tell him."

"Oh, no, ma'am." Focusing on the screen, I typed the first word I could think of. "He wasn't. Nobody else has come in yet. And Barb always says conversation is an integral service of the library."

"I'm glad to hear that. Barb has told me how pleased she is with your work. She would hate for anything to ruin it."

*But you wouldn't.* I only said, "Yes, ma'am."

"We need to leave." Mrs. O'Neil led her husband like a prisoner as he shuffled out the door.

In the seven months that I'd worked at the library in Wellesville and talked to Terry, I couldn't imagine him plotting to murder a woman, even one who was blackmailing him because she was carrying his child.

But I could see his wife doing it. No problem.

<><><>

Once the afternoon turned to evening, I flipped on the flame in the gas fireplace. The fire and the light from the wall sconces dulled the harsh glare of the overhead fixtures. Why did every public place have to be lit like an operating room? Nobody needed to see the lint in the carpet or the bumps in the drywall.

Crouching in front of the shelves holding magazines, I pulled out the oldest issues. Junior high kids lounged around the couches by the fireplace, playing on their phones, killing time until their parents came home from work. If I was going to capture with my camera the cozy atmosphere the fireplace and books created, I'd clear out the kids, add some soft throws, and place a parent and child on a couch, snuggled around a book.

No, better than cozy. Go for mysterious. Turn off the overhead lights. Have three or four friends huddled around an ancient book opened on the coffee table, discovering—

A pair of snug gray corduroy pants hovering at just the right height above black loafers blocked my view. My gaze traveled up to a black sweater with a subtle swirling pattern and the million-watt smile of Jason Carlisle. That smile made him look a lot younger than thirty-seven.

With a stack of novels and picture books under one arm, he said, "I was just talking to Barb. She says you're one of the best hires she's made since she became director. We hope you'll stay."

I got to my feet, meeting his eye level. You wouldn't know he was a member of the library board or belonged to Marlin County's wealthiest family. He talked to everyone, even the high school kids who did the shelving, like they were the most important employees at the library.

"I'm planning on it, sir," I said. "I really like my job."

"It's Jason. Remember?"

Besides being fashionable enough for a runway, Jason had dark brown hair, gel sculpting every strand into place, and soft brown eyes that held a warmth I wanted to wrap myself in. If he was a few inches taller and more muscular, he'd make a perfect Superman.

"Sylvie!" He turned about, and a preschooler with his eyes and bouncing brown curls took hold of his hand. "Rae, are you coming to the library Christmas party? Family is welcome. Or a date."

I slid a magazine into its proper position. "I don't have a family. And I haven't been in Wellsville long enough to find anyone to date."

"I'm surprised the boys around here haven't found you." He flashed his grin.

He was just being nice. At 5'11", my height works against me when it comes to attracting guys. That and my face. My eyes are okay—dark chocolate brown with a slight tilt—but my face is too bony, all cheekbones and chin.

I racked my brain to keep the conversation going. "Is Allison at piano practice?"

Chuckling, Jason changed his grip on Sylvie's hand. "We're that predictable, aren't we? Yes, Richard, Sylvie, and I are waiting here until we have to pick up Allison." He glanced at the clock behind the check-out desk. "We should leave now. Richard!"

His six-year-old son was nowhere to be seen among the chairs, couches, tables, and tween-agers.

Frowning, Jason deposited his books on a table. "He probably went back to the children's room."

"Would you like me to get him? Or watch Sylvie while you get him?"

"That's very nice of you. Sylvie, you stay here." He put her tiny hand in my big, knobby one and walked out of the room.

I knelt beside Sylvie, who stared at me with her finger in her mouth.

"Did you steal sugar?" I said, like my mom did when I was little. I tickled Sylvie on her tummy.

She giggled and batted my hand away.

"If you laugh, you stole sugar." I tickled her again.

Giggling louder, she dashed past me.

I spun on my heels to grab her. She ran to a tall, thin man, who was brushing snow off his leather jacket in the entrance.

He swung her up into his arms "Where's your daddy? Or are you out by yourself for a night on the town?"

"Your brother is hunting for Richard, sir," I said as I approached.

"He'll find him lost in a dinosaur book." He studied me. "You're Rae Riley, right? Barb's talked about you."

Rick Carlisle was several inches taller than his younger brother but shared the same dark hair and eyes. His sharp face, etched with grooves, always wore a strictly serious expression, like the responsibility of being owner and editor-in-chief of the local newspaper prevented him from enjoying anything. Even as he hugged his niece and she snuggled into his shoulder, his mouth stayed a grim, straight line. He'd make a good Batman to his brother's Superman.

"I've liked reading your articles about the roses the sheriff has found at the old children's home."

Rick cocked an eyebrow. "You read the paper? You must be the only person under thirty-five who does."

Jason appeared in the lobby with Richard, his double, minus the hair gel.

"Have you seen this one, Rae?" Richard ran over to me with an open book. "It has conchoraptor and paralititan and a lot of other dinosaurs you don't find in books."

"I saw it. I meant to tell you about it."

Rick carried Sylvie over to his brother.

Jason scooped up their books. "I didn't know you had a date with Barb tonight."

"Why should you know when I have a date?" Rick kissed Sylvie on her curls and passed her over to her father.

"Almost everybody in town knows before you do." Jason's grin took on an ornery slant.

"When I moved back here," Rick massaged a temple, "I'd forgotten nosiness was one of the less charming aspects of small town life."

"People are nosy everywhere."

"True, but in the city, they hide it better." Rick rubbed Richard on the head and then strode to the back of the building where the offices were.

Kneeling again, I stole peeks as Jason got his books checked out and hustled his kids into their winter gear.

He was such a nice guy. He even had full custody of his kids, which said something about him. And his ex-wife. Or maybe it only said that being a Carlisle in Wellesville, Ohio, gave you a big advantage in divorce court.

Still…

Richard held the door open as Jason carried Sylvie and a bag straining with books.

They seemed like a nice family to belong to.

<><><>

On Sunday, as I filed out of the small, high-vaulted sanctuary with the rest of the congregation, the small, thin figure of Lydia Malinowski slipped through the flow of people to me. "Rae, are you staying for lunch?"

I stumbled as her youngest grandson pushed past me. "Yes, ma'am."

Mrs. M. swatted at the first grader, but her swing was so slow that her fingers only brushed his strawberry blond hair. "Then sit with us." She smiled up at me with dark blue eyes as still and reassuring as the sea on a windless day.

Mrs. M. was the calmest person I'd ever met. I'd never seen her hurry or heard her raise her voice, even when she scolded her grandkids. Along with several ladies in the church knitting group, Mrs. M. had made me feel welcomed at the Presbyterian church from the first service I had attended, every week asking how I was settling into my job and pushing home-baked bread and canned vegetables on me.

We inched through the line to the buffet, the comforting aroma of chili and chicken noodle soup stoking my hunger. Three slices of plain toast and two pickles hadn't lasted long.

When my turn came, I loaded my plate. I'd eat slow so I could legitimately hang around and pick up any leftovers offered to me. Mom and I had attended many churches as we moved around, but I had never seen one that ate like this.

Mrs. M. and I edged around already-seated members, scouting for empty chairs. If the lights had to be strong in the fellowship hall, then the walls should have been painted something darker than white. I wanted to get my sunglasses out of my truck.

We found spots at a long table in the back. As I lifted my first spoonful of chili, her son, Walter R. Malinowski IV, and three redheaded grandsons joined us. Had the sheriff's late wife been a redhead? His boys certainly didn't take after him.

Taking a seat across from me, the sheriff nodded at me and dug in. He was one of the few people I'd met who made me feel short. Close to six-six, with biceps bulging like pumpkins under a rumpled button-down shirt, he could easily become the next Thor if he grew out his blond crewcut and added a beard.

Of the three men, Mr. Malinowski was the hardest to start a conversation with. I came armed with questions to kick things off. "Sheriff, since I'm not twenty-one and can't buy a handgun, what gun do you recommend for protection at my apartment?"

His eyes, the color of his mother's, flew open, and he gulped a chunk of bread. "Don't you feel safe in Wellsville?"

I stirred my soup. "I live alone."

"Wellsville isn't exactly Chicago."

"You seem to think so, Mal," said Mrs. M.

No one I had met, including his own mother, called him "Walter."

"The way you go on in those articles in the paper," Mrs. M. buttered a roll, "you'd think someone had committed murder at the old children's home instead of just trespassing."

That gave me the perfect opening. "Wasn't somebody murdered there? Bella Rydell?"

"Josh Dixon says," Aaron, the sheriff's middle son with dusty orange hair, spewed crumbs, "his cousin's girlfriend's brother saw her ghost."

"Close your mouth." His dad forked lettuce. "Don't listen to Josh Dixon. Or his cousin's girlfriend's brother."

"Nobody died at the home." Mrs. M. patted Aaron's arm. "A woman was never seen again in town after the night of the fire, but that doesn't mean she died in it."

Leaning against the sheriff, Micah, the strawberry blond, tipped his head back to catch his father's eye. "Is that circumspecial evidence, Dad?"

"No, that's jumping to conclusions."

"But still," said Rusty, the oldest, his voice squeaking as it tried out its new, deeper register, "it seems like a ginormous coincidence that somebody disappeared the same night of a ginormous fire." He had the most gorgeous shade of dark red hair, like autumn oak leaves. I knew girls who would die for—or was it dye for?—a color like that.

"I can see why people thought so." Mrs. M. chewed on a bite of salad, staring out over church members enjoying their lunches. "Bella made life pretty comfortable for herself in Marlin County by going after men with money."

The sheriff sat up straighter, glancing at his sons. "Ma, I don't think now is a good time to—"

"Why would she leave almost everything in her apartment? The paper said it looked like she left in a hurry. Or died."

"Ma," Mal scratched at an eyebrow, "kids are present."

"You are so protective." She squeezed his catcher's mitt of a hand. "But, sweetie, the boys have heard much worse whenever the Tomiches show up for the service and decide to share during joys and concerns."

"I'm not a baby, Dad." Rusty stabbed a cucumber. "I'm in seventh grade."

"And there are still things you don't need to know," his father said. "If Bella died, she did not die at the children's home. Not a single bone or tooth of any kind was found. Remember, Ma?"

"Of course, sweetie. I'm surprised you do. Oh, I bet you read the original reports. At the time, all you thought about was going to college to play football. And everything else a senior has to deal with. You were—you were—what's the word?—preoccupied that year."

With my mother blackmailing him, little wonder he was preoccupied. Or was he preoccupied with planning her murder?

"Did you play in the NFL?" I said. In old yearbooks, I had discovered Mal had been a star lineman.

"Didn't make it that far."

I scooted back. His baritone was pretty powerful for just one-on-one conversation, but sometimes he seemed to forget he was indoors and not issuing orders to deputies at a busy intersection.

He drained his cup of iced tea. "Busted my knee to pieces my sophomore year. That was a blessing, though. I'm a better cop than a football player."

As we polished off our lunch, Mrs. M. told me that she knew

of no one who'd mourned Bella going missing or could explain the appearance of a rose on each of the first five anniversaries after the fire. But the roses confirmed people's suspicions that someone died in the fire.

Gathering his paper products, the sheriff recommended a couple of guns. "In town, you're better off with a dog."

"A dog would cost more money, I think, in the long run."

He frowned. "If you get one, I can show you how not to kill yourself with it." He gave me his number.

I fished out my phone and punched it in.

"That's our land line. We don't have reception at the farm." He walked toward the garbage can. "Ma can tell you when I'm available." With his plate poised over the can, he paused and then jerked his head to me. "You know Ma and me live together, don't you? She'll be there. And my boys. And possibly my sister. And her husband. And their kids. You can't spit without hitting a Malinowski in this county."

"Yes, sir, I know. Your mom told me. Thanks for letting me come over." He didn't need to worry about coming across as a creep. He and Jason and Terry treated me like the male teachers in my high school—kind or helpful or friendly, but nothing else.

I went to the kitchen to help with clean up. Could someone go from an almost-murderer to a police officer? I couldn't imagine anybody raised by Mrs. M. turning evil.

Once the kitchen was clean and back in order, I walked to my pickup through an icy shower loaded with enough left-over soup, salad, and bread to last me until Wednesday.

Settling into the cab of my truck, I turned the key and didn't shift. The stick wouldn't budge.

I pressed my head against the steering wheel. Not again.

"Hey!"

Jumping, I knocked my knees against the dash.

Micah Malinowski popped up outside my window. "Your truck stuck again?"

He was so cute. Put a pointy red hat on him, and he could pass for a Christmas elf.

"Yeah." I blew a long strand of hair off my lips.

My pickup was gaining a reputation as a piece of junk, which it was. Most Sunday services ended with some male member of the congregation crawling under my truck to unjam the gears.

"Hey, Dad!" Micah waved at his father, who was opening the door of a red SUV for his mom. "Rae's gears are all stuck!"

As the shower turned into a downpour, Mrs. M. smiled and said something to the sheriff. The left side of his face scrunched in a grimace, like he'd noticed a stone in his shoe. Her smile straining, Mrs. M. elbowed him.

I sucked in my cheeks. I couldn't burst out laughing if Mal was coming to help me. But I'd never seen a movie yet where Thor's mother had to shove her son into action.

A sigh raised and lowered his boulder-size shoulders, and the sheriff trudged toward my truck.

<><><>

Standing in a thicket near the edge of the woods, I studied the shell that used to be the children's home and the weedy field that used to be the yard. No cops.

The early morning sunshine made the bare tree limbs look a little less threatening but held no warmth a week before Christmas.

Crunching through the brittle bushes as thorns tugged at my down vest and jeans jacket, I locked my attention on the home. Still no—wait!

I dropped behind a fallen tree, cradling my camera.

Something moved past an empty window, right beside the fireplace. Something tall.

A gust of wind spun dead leaves into my face, but I kept my gaze glued to the building.

A man climbed out the back window I usually used.

Rick Carlisle. He tugged the brim of his hat lower and tromped into the woods.

Why was he sneaking around the children's home? I stayed behind the log, waiting for his footsteps to disappear. Was he working on a story for the paper? But one of his employees could be assigned to snoop. And he was snooping. Like me, he parked his vehicle nowhere near the home.

After the last footstep faded, I waited several more minutes. Then I raced to the building and slipped in the window.

I scrutinized the room. The usual garbage cluttered the floor—beer cans, food wrappers, crumpled leaves. Mr. Carlisle hadn't disturbed anything. I laid the last two roses in the grate, and in two minutes, tore my way through thorns and brambles to the dirt road where I'd parked my pickup.

As I stepped out onto the road, brushing twigs off my leggings, I skidded to a halt.

A patrol SUV was pulled up in front of my truck, and the sheriff stood next to it, his back to me.

"Rae!" His bellow shocked a flock of crows into flight.

I remained motionless. He hadn't seen me. I could duck back into the woods. But I needed my pickup. I was on opening shift at the library.

"Hey, Sheriff." I sauntered down the middle of the road, my camera bouncing against my side.

Mal spun around. "Is your truck broken down?"

"No." I held up my camera. "I wanted to take advantage of the sunrise."

"Out here?" He rested his hand on the butt of his gun, appearing even bigger in his black uniform. "If you're going to take pictures along deserted country roads, get a dog."

"I haven't had any trouble." I unlocked my truck and swung the door open.

His dark blue eyes narrowing, Mal put his broad hand on the top of my door. "You had better not have been poking around the old home."

Was he talking as a police officer or a would-be killer? I rose up on my toes, digging in, every muscle coiling.

Not a sound of anyone else around. Even the wind was gone.

I met his glare. "I know if I did that, I'd be trespassing."

"You'd better know that." He released the door and stalked to his car. "Somebody's gonna get killed there if the county doesn't tear that place down."

I sank back to my heels. How was I going to confront three possible killers when I panicked facing just one?

Mal had one leg in his SUV, then lowered it to the ground. "When you come out to the farm this weekend for your shooting lesson, bring your camera. We've got a lot of land. With woods and a creek. And my sister's place backs up to ours on the south side, so you could go over there, too. Jeanine and Hank won't care."

He'd switched from intimidation to invitation so fast, my tongue couldn't react. I nodded, then slid behind the peeling steering wheel. Maybe sensing it was almost Christmas, my truck gave me the gift of actually shifting.

Mal followed me. I hunched over the wheel, stretching my neck from side to side to release the last cramps of tension.

*Mom, I know this is what you spent your whole life protecting me from. But I've got to know. I've got to.*

Three new stamped envelopes lay on the passenger seat. If Mal left me soon, I could drive to the post office out in Barton and mail them before my shift. Leaving anonymous text messages would have been easier, if I could've found Mal's number, but since I already had their business addresses from the letters Mom wrote, going old school seemed the best route.

Mal turned away at the first light in Wellsville. I wound through a few back streets and drove out of town. Mom had thought snail mail the safest way to deliver her letters. And I could not take any chance that the three men might figure out who was accusing them of attacking Bella Rydell.

**<><><>**

Okay. I couldn't stay on my phone the whole time. No one else was.

Sliding my phone into my purse, I pressed against a wall as the library staff and their families chatted and snacked in the meeting room I had helped Barb and Jill, the assistant director, decorate, but the fake evergreen garland and tinsel strung across the ceiling couldn't dress up the blank, beige room.

I shouldn't have come. Not alone. "Awkward" didn't even touch my anxiety at being the only person flying solo. Even Barb had brought Rick Carlisle as her date.

"Hello, Rae!" Carrying a cup of punch, Terry weaved around Jill and her husband. "You look very nice this evening."

Strange comment. I was wearing what I usually did since the cold weather set in, leggings and a sweater. "Uh—thanks." I munched on a cracker, catching the slightest scent of alcohol. Maybe Terry had started partying at his house because he knew we wouldn't have alcohol in the library.

He edged closer, the scent growing stronger. "Have you had a chance to watch—"

"Terence." Mrs. O'Neil appeared at his side. "Rick wants to speak to you." She had her back to me.

"Oh, okay." Terry winked. "Merry Christmas, Rae." He followed his wife, staggering as he dodged a pack of kids who thundered past.

Terry, along with Jason and Mal, had to have received my anonymous notes by now. If the accusation was worrying Terry, he hid it completely. Or the alcohol did.

Jason's oldest daughter, Allison darted past me and sat at the table Barb and I had set up with coloring sheets and crafts for the kids. She chose a picture of a Christmas tree and a green marker, then began coloring it with precise strokes.

Standing behind her, I said, "You're very neat. That looks professional."

Turning huge brown eyes to me, she beamed. "Thank you." She held up a red marker. "Want to help?"

I grabbed a chair. At least this gave me something to do besides pretend I was a wall decoration. "What do you want for Christmas?"

"Soap."

My marker skidded over a line. "Soap?"

She peered at my mistake. "Slow down. Stay within the lines."

"Sorry. Why do you want soap?"

"I want to learn how to make really good smelling soap."

Other kids joined us, choosing pictures or assembling ornaments. I asked them about their Christmas wish list, trying to ignore the burnt-up feeling that hollowed me out. This was the second Christmas I wasn't expecting any gifts. Several families from church had invited me to dinner on Christmas Eve or Christmas Day and would probably give me something, but only so I wouldn't feel left out, not because they knew me.

Allison pulled a picture of elves out of the stack. "Do you want to do this one?"

"Okay. How about purple elves? Just to be different."

"Good thinking."

Bending my head over the sheet, I snatched glimpses of Jason and Terry.

Jason's Hollywood smile was absent unless he was talking to one of his kids. Even then it only lasted a few seconds.

Terry lunged from one knot of people to the next, laughing, throwing out his arms in gestures so big that the people he was speaking to backed up.

His wife, parked beside the buffet table, watched his every move, her lips tightening, her knuckles whitening around her glass of punch.

My attention shifted to Rick Carlisle. His serious expression looked strained, like he was fighting a migraine.

What had he been doing at the home?

Allison and I finished her picture, and I left to get more appetizers. Despite the scorched feeling in my gut, I wanted to take advantage of the free food. If I ate enough, I wouldn't have to fix supper when I got to the apartment.

Joining me at the table, Jason said in a low voice, "May I speak to you, Rae?"

Standing up perfectly straight, I forced down a cheese cube and smiled. "For sure." It was the first time all evening Jason had talked to me.

We walked into the hall, and Jason whispered, "I wanted you to know that if anyone bothers you on the job, you should tell Barb and me immediately. Barb thinks you have great potential and wouldn't want to lose you."

My eyebrows drew together. "Mr.—Jason, no one has bothered me. Except Mr. Olsen, and Barb says he's mean to everybody."

"Good. Glad to hear it." He grabbed at Sylvie as she ran by us. "Just remember—you can always trust Barb and me to help you."

Lifting Sylvie, he went back into the room.

I bit into another cube of cheddar. Where had that come from? I set down my plate and walked down the hall to the bathroom. I still had no clue when I opened the stall door to leave and found Mrs. O'Neil waiting for me by the sinks.

"Stay away from my husband." She spat the order.

I tottered back against the toilet. "Pardon?"

"You're no innocent." She moved in. "If you want to keep your job, you stay away from him." Her glare seemed ready to spear me. "Understand?"

If I agreed, maybe she'd go. My head bobbed up and down as I steadied myself with a hand on the toilet paper dispenser.

"You had better." She wheeled around and marched—I had never seen her merely walk—to the door, flung it open, and click-clacked down the hall.

Sagging in the open stall, I clutched at the top of the door. Maybe she'd been complaining about me, and Jason had heard.

I wasn't the mood now for coloring or snacking or small talk or pretending I didn't feel naked without some sort of relative or date.

On shaking knees, I crossed to the closed door. I'd say my good-byes, see if I could snag some food to take with me, and take off. I had a lot to get ready anyway.

Just not for Christmas.

<><><>

My phone read 2:57 a.m. Terry had better be on time. Waiting all through Christmas Eve alone had shredded my nerves.

Clicking on the flashlight, I laid it on the dirt floor of the home. I didn't need that much light to see. The almost full moon radiated into the roofless building, revealing even the details of the corners in an otherworldly silver sheen, like the home and all the land outside was bathed in a fairy spell. If only I could set up my camera.

I crossed to an empty window opposite from the front door. Maybe I should have accepted all those invitations from church members. But I'd thought I wouldn't make good company. I hadn't even gone to Christmas Eve service because I was too worked up to sit still.

Climbing out, I stepped over my rifle lying on the ground under the sill. At least, no die-hard ghost hunters had decided to camp out to catch a glimpse of the ghost of Bella Rydell on the twentieth anniversary of her death. The holiday and the cold probably took care of them.

Shaking feeling into my hands, I fingered Mom's letters, folded in my pocket. The cold penetrated through my layers of down vest, jeans jacket, and two sweaters, sinking into my skin like thousands of tiny, icy fangs.

The whoosh of a vehicle on the road made me turn. It grew louder. Headlights shone on the back wall and then vanished. A door opened, shut. After a few steps as frostbitten grass bent and broke beneath his weight, Terry appeared in the doorway.

"Who's here? I can't pay you. I didn't kill anybody."

Dressed in a long coat and driving cap, he swept a flashlight over the walls.

"Stay where you are." I leaped down to the trash-covered floor.

"Rae?" My name was only a breath.

"Yes, Terry."

His face contorted, hardened, into a scowl so fierce that with the beam coming from the flashlight on the floor, he could have passed for a serial killer in a suspense thriller. "Have you been leaving the roses out here? How did you know I'd left them years ago? Did that make you think I killed Bella?'

One mystery solved, sort of. "Yes. I left the roses, so when I wrote my notes, y'all would take me seriously. I hoped the two roses would signal I knew Bella Rydell was pregnant." I flexed my stiff fingers. "I didn't know you left the roses the first time."

With a gloved hand, he rubbed his beard hard enough to scrub it off. "I can't pay you, no matter how much you want. My wife would know."

"I didn't ask for money in my note."

"Why else did you want to talk to me out here?" His gaze searched me from the soles of my cracked boots to my blue knit hat. "How did you know Bella Rydell was pregnant?"

Like I was throwing off all my clothes, I said, "I'm her daughter."

"What?" Again the word was just air. He backed away, his heavy cheeks trembling under his beard. "That doesn't mean you're mine. Where's Bella?"

My heart dropped like a bird shot out of the sky. "She died of cancer, right before I turned eighteen." If that was his attitude, I prayed he was right. "Twenty years ago, someone sent my mom a note without signing it, asking her to meet him here at 11 p.m. on Christmas Eve. The note mentioned the baby so Mom knew only one of three men could have sent it -- the three men she was blackmailing."

"I wasn't the only one?" He whipped off his cap. "I'm not surprised."

Tears fought to surface, but I squinted against them. "When my mom came to the home, she was hit over the head from behind. She never saw who it was. When she woke up, the whole building was burning. She made it out."

"It wasn't me." The professor slapped back on his hat. "I was in Canton, visiting my wife's family. Like I did tonight. Like I've done every Christmas Eve for," the anger dissolved from his face, and his shoulders slumped, "the last forty-two years."

Was it true? It would be hard for me to check, but after seeing his wife in attack mode, it would take someone with more nerve than Terry had ever shown to get out of visiting his in-laws to commit a crime.

"I believe you." My voice held a firmness that surprised me.

"And I'm not your father." He said this very loud, as if the volume would change his words to truth. "Even if DNA testing proved I was, I couldn't acknowledge you."

"I understand." Better than he realized. I took a card out of the back pocket of my jeans. "I have a blood donor card. My blood type's rare. If you know yours, we may be able to settle this right now."

Another searing stare. But I met it, standing as still as the Arctic air around us.

"I'm O positive," he said.

*Thank You, Heavenly Father.*

Tossing the card like a Frisbee, I stepped back. "I'm AB negative. An O parent can't have an AB child."

He stooped to pick up the card and turned his flashlight on it. Then he dropped the card and walked backwards. "I'm going. If you tell anyone I was involved with Bella, I'll tell them you're lying. Anyone in the county will believe me over you."

"I know, sir." I sent up another thanks. "I have one more thing." Pulling an envelope from the pocket of my vest, I checked the name. "My mom became a Christian after she escaped the fire. She realized how awful her life had become and knew she needed saved. Right before she died, she wrote three letters to each of the men she tried to blackmail, asking him to forgive her. She wanted to—"

"Forgive her?" Terry threw back his head and laughed, the ugly noise bouncing off the stones.

Crushing the envelope in my outstretched hand, I shuddered.

"After what she did to me? She zeroed in on me and wouldn't stop until she had me panting for her like a dog in heat. Being married to Melissa, she knew I couldn't resist. Then she demanded money from me, or she'd tell the whole town and the officials at the college that the baby was mine." He laughed again.

*Shut up. Just shut up and go.* I drew back my hand.

"Give me that letter." He lunged toward me.

Flinging away the ball of paper, I ran to the window and laid my hand on the gun.

But Terry was bending over to pick up the ball. He dug out his lighter, then flicked the flame to life and held the envelope over it.

Another fire in the old home to burn evidence.

When the envelope fell to the dirt as flaming wisps, he closed the lighter and walked to the door.

As much as I wanted to see the back of him, I had to ask, "Why did you leave the roses?"

He turned halfway to me, his posture collapsing even more than when his wife ordered him around. "I thought Bella died in the fire. If she was alive, she still would have wanted the money. And if the baby was mine, somebody should mourn it." The scowl returned. "It was stupid. The kids who partied here noticed the rose and wanted to find out who was leaving it. I was nearly caught the last time. So I quit." He heaved himself out of the doorway.

"That was kind of you." My voice sounded as empty as the building.

Without looking back, he said, "It was stupid."

He trudged through the snow, got in his car, and drove away.

<><><>

Sinking to my knees, I let the tears go and bawled, bawled until my eyes were too cold to release another drop.

What made me think even if my father wasn't the attacker, he'd want me? He wouldn't want everyone in Marlin County to know he'd had an affair with the town tramp. How could I have been so stupid? I should have mailed the letters like Mom wanted.

Doubled over on the dirt, I clutched my stomach, tears blazing tracks down my icy cheeks. The cold ate up through my jeans, numbing my legs.

*Heavenly Father, I need an earthly father. If I don't get one…*

A vehicle ground up the snow-clogged drive.

I scrambled to the window on the back wall and threw myself out. Whipping out my phone, I checked the time. 3:32 a.m.

Wiping my cheeks, I took quivering breaths. I had to go through with the next interview.

Two car doors slammed.

I lowered my phone. Jason wouldn't have brought someone.

Would he?

But Jason and Rick Carlisle, wearing snug ski jackets and black ski caps, entered through the doorway, flashlights in their hands.

"Stop right there!" I jumped into the building.

"Rae!" Jason's jaw swung loose. "What's going on?" Despite light from three flashlights, I couldn't read Jason's expression clearly, but his eyes looked red-rimmed.

"You aren't blackmailing my brother for something he didn't do." Rick shouted at me like I was standing out on the road. He squared himself to me. "I murdered Bella Rydell, and Jason didn't know until yesterday."

The rest of me went numb, but not from the weather. Even my brain. What?

"We came to tell you your greedy demands don't matter." He lifted his chin. "Because as soon as we're done here, I'm going to Mal to confess everything."

"Rae," Jason squinted at me, "how did you know about me and Bella and—and everything?"

"I'm her baby." As the brothers' eyes almost grew out of their sockets, I told them the story I'd started with Terry.

"Once Mom escaped, she was so scared. She hid out in a barn for a few days, then sneaked into her apartment, took some clothes and money, and hitchhiked to Columbus. She felt safe enough there to go to a hospital. A nurse there was a Christian and helped my mom get saved."

"But—but," Rick rubbed the back of his neck, "that means I didn't kill anybody."

"No, sir. You didn't."

Jason grabbed his brother by the shoulders. "You didn't commit murder! You didn't do it!"

Rick shook his head as if it weighed a thousand pounds. "All these years…" He dragged his gaze to meet mine. "You know, it's not committing the sin that gets to you. It's living with it."

I had to know the whole story. "You tried to kill my mom to help your brother?"

"Jason told me as soon as Bella claimed she was carrying his baby and wanted money." Rick spoke quietly, as if his mind was only partially concerned with his words. "We didn't have as much money then as people thought. Our dad had recently died and left a lot of debt."

He barked a bitter laugh. "Over the years, I tried to justify what I did, lying to myself that it would kill my mom to get caught in a scandal, it would ruin Jason's life. But I did it," his body grew so taut, it trembled along with his voice, "because I hated that little scrap of trash for trying to control us." The trembling stopped, and he seemed to shrink. "I told myself I would make up for it. Help people out. That's why I took over the paper and used it to advocate for people who needed it. But in the past year, I realized I could never make up for it." His arms flopped against his sides. "I don't care who knows it now."

I blinked. I stared. I blinked some more. During the thousands of times I had imagined how these meetings would play out, I had never guessed at this reality.

I shoved my hands into my vest's pockets, and paper rattled.

Pulling out the letters, I read the names and held out the right one. "You need to read this, both of you. My mom wrote—"

"What is going on here?" The booming voice of Sheriff Malinowski made us jump as his massive frame filled the doorway, gun drawn.

"Bella didn't die in the fire!" Jason shouted.

"Of course she didn't." He stepped down to the ground, wearing a camo jacket and hunting cap instead of his uniform. "Rae. I knew you weren't out here just for a photo op."

Heaving a huge sigh, Rick gave me a feeble smile. "You must have really thought Jason was guilty since you called Mal to back you up."

"That's not why he's—"

"Mal," Rick planted himself in front of the sheriff, "I tried to murder Bella and her unborn child and then started the fire here to cover my crime."

Mal's eyebrows crept up his forehead. "You did?"

I said, "But Mal can't arrest you."

"I can't?"

Rick spun to me. "What do you know?"

"In the state of Ohio, the statute of limitations on almost all violent crimes, except murder and aggravated murder, is twenty years. It's now twenty years and one day since you committed the crime." I handed him Mom's letter. "You need to read this, Mr.

Carlisle."

His fingers fumbling, Rick grasped the letter.

Taking out the last envelope, I said, "Sheriff, this one's for you."

Jason looked wildly from Mal to me and back again. "You mean Bella was—"

"Blackmailing both of you about me." I told Mal the whole story of Mom's escape and salvation. "She was always afraid her attacker would find us and finish the job. We moved all the time and never came back to Ohio. When she saved up enough money, Mom even had our names legally changed."

Shifting my feet to use up the adrenaline that was building in me, I wanted to ask them about their blood types. I hurried through my explanation. "She felt horrible for what she had done. She hoped you would forgive her."

"She forgives me," Rick whispered, his hands falling limply.

Jason snatched the letter from his brother's grip as Rick teetered beside him.

"She also wanted her attacker to know that she forgave him." I clenched and unclenched my hands. "It's in all your letters because she didn't know which one of you was guilty."

"She forgives me." Rick fingered his lip. "But—but why? I tried to burn her up."

"Mom said you were no worse than she was. She was ready to abort me as soon as she got the blackmail money."

"And-and-and—" Mal cleared his throat "—you deliberately picked Christmas Day because it was after the statute of limitations?"

"Yes, sir. Mom had mentioned that she didn't know if her attacker could be prosecuted because of the time that had passed. I did some research and decided this is the way she'd want me to do it since I wasn't going to mail the letters like she asked me. As far as she was concerned, this was between her, her attacker and God."

Rick moaned like he'd taken a fatal blow and dropped to the floor. Then he drew up his knees and sobbed into his folded arms.

"Is she right, Mal?" Tears slid along Jason's nose. "Have the statute of limitations run out?"

"Hang on a minute." The sheriff stepped over to me. "Did either one of them threaten you?"

Jason flung out his arms. "Of course not, Mal. We wouldn't --"

"I'm talking to Rae." My name came out as a snarl so fierce Jason reared back. Mal softened his voice. "Did either of them threaten you in any way?"

I described exactly what happened, pumping my knees in place, the icy fabric scraping them. They had to stop questioning me so I could question them.

Mal pushed up the brim of his hunting cap. "Since no crime has been committed tonight, except flagrant trespassing, Rick's in the clear." He shook his head. "I can't believe Rick did... I've known him for years." He held up his note. "And Bella. To forgive that. And to ask for forgiveness -- your mom had some kind of guts."

A lump bobbed in my throat. "She did."

A bone-cold quiet settled on us as Rick's sobs subsided.

I couldn't wait a second more. "Do you know your blood types?" I pulled out my card and held it in both hands like a shield. "I have a blood donor card, so you know I'm not making it up. I have a rare type. We might be able to figure out which one of you is my father."

"We wouldn't think you would lie to us, Rae." Jason brushed his cheeks. "I'm O positive."

"AB negative," said Mal.

All my AB negative blood rushed up my neck and throbbed in my temples as I whispered, "An O parent can't have an AB child."

Jason's face drooped with his whole body as the sheriff gasped, "Oh, my...oh – holy smoke!" Pocketing his gun, he fell back against a wall.

A tear slid to my chapped lips. I'd dropped so many that I didn't bother to wipe it away. "I'm – I'm sorry."

"N-n-no." Mal bent over, clutching his knees. "You don't have to – just give me a minute. It's – it's – holy smoke!"

"He's not upset, Rae." Jason walked over to me and took my hands in his. "He's happily shocked. Right, Mal?"

The sheriff wagged his head in agreement, dragging in a bucketful of air and releasing it in a huge cloud.

Jason said, "He's just trying not to pass out."

"Sh-sh-shut up, Carlisle."

For the first time that night, a hint of Jason's usual grin eased the tense lines of his face. "Did you know Mal and I graduated from the same class? We've known each other since kindergarten."

"I saw that in an old yearbook at the library." I bit my lip. Bent over, Mal didn't look happy.

"Thank you, Rae." Jason lifted my hands. "You could have ignored your mother's desire and tried to get revenge or justice. But you saved my brother. He's my best friend. I don't know—" he choked on his words "—what I'd do without him."

"Thank my mom. I only did what I promised her."

Raising his face to the star-scattered sky and glowing moon, Jason shouted, "Thank you, Bella! Thank You, God!" He squeezed my gloved fingers. "If you ever need anything, anything at all," the mega-watt smile flashed into brilliance, "think of me as your fairy godfather."

I gulped. "For sure."

With a great inhale, Mal pushed off the wall. "You and Rick can leave."

Gathering his brother into his arms, Jason hoisted Rick onto his feet. His face tear-stained and blank, Rick didn't seem to notice.

Jason said, "You're a lucky guy, Malinowski."

"Not lucky. Blessed."

My heart soared to the moon, raising me to my toes.

*Heavenly Father, he wants me!*

Swaying, Mal reached back with one hand for the wall. He didn't say a word until we heard Jason's engine turn over. "Do you understand the risk you took tonight, Rae? Even if the statute of limitations had run out, Rick may have wanted to keep his crime a secret."

I ran—really skipped— to the empty window and retrieved the rifle. "If I had trouble, I brought this. I was going to call 911 and hold him."

Resting his hands on his knees again, Mal chuckled. "And I showed you how to use it. What if I'd been the criminal and didn't want anyone to know?"

"I'd either have to shoot it out with you or run."

Gulping another load of frozen air, he said, "And you did all this—the roses, the letters, getting to know us—to find out who attacked your mom?"

"To find my father and figure out if he attacked my mom."

"I thought you were dead." He clamped a hand on top of his cap as if he was afraid it would fly off. "When Bella didn't contact me on New Year's Day to collect the money, I thought she must have died in the fire. And you too. It was only when I got into law enforcement that I realized conditions have to be just right for a fire to destroy all traces of a body. That's when I guessed Bella must have decided I wasn't going to come through with the $5,000 and took off and aborted you. That's what she said she'd do if I didn't pay."

"She asked for $5,000?"

"Yeah. Bella must have assumed I'd gotten cash from my football scholarship. I don't know why else she'd think a farm kid whose mom worked as a cook at an elementary school would have that kind of money." His lips drew into a tight frown. "Over the years, I told myself it wasn't likely you were mine. I'd only been with Bella once. Here. After the first football game of my senior year. But deep down," he squeezed his eyes shut, "I knew you were mine, and you were dead." He pressed his palms into his sockets, rapidly releasing vapor clouds.

I inched forward, back, forward. What could I say? How do you talk to a newly found father? "Well, now you know the truth."

He didn't move, breathing like each inhale was his last.

Could I offer some daughterly advice? "Do you want to sit down? In your car where it's warm? The heater doesn't work in my truck."

"Along with the gears." He removed his hands and wobbled to the doorway.

Carrying the rifle, I trotted by his side. "Do you need any help?"

"No, no." He waved away the offer. "I'll be fine. I'm feeling –" Mal lurched to a stop. He turned, the left side of his mouth hitching a fraction. "I'm feeling like maybe I do."

He was just being nice. But it was the nicest sort of nice.

Like I was made of glass, he laid an arm across my shoulders. I slid my arm along the small of his back. It felt weird but right. And stiff under his coat.

Was it a brace? Or maybe ... "You wore your bullet-proof vest?"

"I didn't know what I was walking into," Mal said.

We climbed up and through the doorway.

The bright moonlight touched everything—bare trees, seared grasses, the home, us—with a silver glow. I could believe animals spoke on a Christmas Eve like this. Or I could find a father who actually wanted to claim me.

Mal looked up, his lips moving without a sound. I lifted up my prayer with his.

"I am so sorry." His subdued tone was so quiet that he sounded like a different person. "I shouldn't have assumed you died. Once I realized there was a chance Bella wasn't dead, I should have tried to track her --"

"No. No, if you had tried to find us, Mom would have thought you attacked her and were trying to finish the job. She would have run even faster. I don't blame you. I gave up blaming her."

Both sides of his mouth joined in the smile. "You got some kind of guts."

I didn't think it was possible, but my heart flew even higher. "Do you still feel faint?"

"No." He answered too fast. "Just a little light-headed." We began walking. "People don't come back from the dead. And on Christmas."

My truck, the only vehicle in sight, still looked decrepit even gilded in moonlight. "Where's your car?"

"Oh, yeah." Mal stumbled, and we halted. "I came early to check over the situation. Parked down the road a ways." He leaned on me more than I expected, and I locked my knees. "We've got a bit of a hike."

"I don't care." I wanted to run and turn cartwheels. But I stayed by his side. "Do you think your boys will like me?"

"Of course. Once they get to know you. Ma already thinks you're -- Ma!" Taking his weight off my shoulders, he patted his pockets with his free hand. "She's gonna kill me!"

The laugh burst out of me, and I dropped the rifle to throw my hand over my mouth.

"What's so funny?" Mal removed his phone from the back pocket of his jeans.

I had to answer. "You sound like you're thirteen."

He rolled his eyes. "Ma can make me feel that way. I still don't know how." Pressing his thumb on the ID button, he said, "I told her I'd call as soon as I learned something. She heard about this whole mess for the first time yesterday. She was beyond stunned. And worried." He put the phone to his ear. "She thought maybe I was being set up, although how anybody who had a grudge against me would know about me and Bella is -- hey, Ma, I'm alive."

Her answer made him pull the phone from his ear. Then he looked down at me, and his face lit up brighter than the moon and all the stars overhead. "Ma, Ma … well, it's a long story, and I can tell you better when I get home. But I knew you wanted the whole family together for supper tonight. So I got your oldest granddaughter with me, and I'm driving her home because you know how unreliable Rae's truck is, and I thought -- "

My dad jerked the phone away again as my grandma whooped like an angel had announced for unto her a granddaughter was born.

# A Mixed Marriage

I'd heard all the warnings from family and friends.

"Mixed marriages are so stressful. Marriage is hard enough without adding a difference in politics/culture/religion/etc."

But none of my nearest and dearest told me the dire results of when a fake Christmas tree fan marries a live Christmas tree fanatic.

I was raised in a live Christmas tree family. From an early age, my dad, my sisters, and I tramped through Christmas tree farms in the wilds of Belmont County, Ohio, searching for the perfect tree. My sisters and I learned to look for a tree with a straight trunk and a minimum of gaps between the branches. By the time we had wrestled it into the living room and managed to get it erect, the tree had always swollen to three times its original size and threatened to engulf the room. My sisters and I also learned how to crawl on our bellies under the lowest branches and avoid the sharp needles to water the tree.

As I grew older, we bought cut trees that were brought to the parking lot of a Lutheran church. In college, fir trees my grandfather had planted had grown big enough to use as Christmas trees, so we saved money for a few years.

The process of finding and placing the tree in our home was an important tradition of our Christmas.

My husband's parents, however, taught him the evils of a live Christmas tree. They were dirty. They shed needles whenever they felt like it. But, above all, live trees were suicidal, happily looking for the nearest spark to immolate themselves and the homes of those foolish enough to take them in.

A fake tree was neat and tame, content to sit in its corner until the Fourth of July if you wanted it to.

Obviously, once we married, we couldn't observe both traditions.

It wasn't an issue for our first two Christmases because we lived in an apartment, and it made sense to decorate the little four-foot fake tree I'd used when I was single.

But the first Christmas in our new house brought our mixed marriage to a crisis.

Our two-story living room begged for a grand tree, towering above the rest of the decorations and presents.

My husband wanted no muss, no fuss, no sad news story about a Christmas Eve house fire.

I wasn't in much of position to argue. I was working full time and seven months pregnant, too tired to put up any kind of a fight, no matter how much I wanted a live tree.

One evening in December, I dragged myself into our home after an exhausting day of work. In the corner of the living room, beside a set of two-story windows, sat a Christmas tree stand.

I don't remember if I laughed or cried. Probably both, in my advanced state of pregnancy. But it was the sweetest gift I've ever received.

We've had only one real crisis since that first Christmas in our new house. When our kids were about four and six, my husband wanted to know why I was so determined to have a live tree. He dug in his heels and insisted on switching to a fake one.

When our four-year-old found out, he announced, "No tree, no presents."

My husband was stunned. A preschooler was willing to give up his Christmas gifts for a live tree? My husband hadn't realized that I'd so thoroughly indoctrinated our kids in my cause.

He graciously gave in to majority rule.

My husband and I now have a compromise. The kids and I tag a tree at a local Christmas tree farm during Thanksgiving weekend. A week before Christmas, we cut it down. My husband gets to complain about putting it up. We take it down on New Year's Day, and my husband gets to complain again.

Will we continue to get a live tree once the kids are living in their own homes? I don't know. The reason I love a live tree is all the ritual and work surrounding it. It would be no fun at all to pick out a Christmas tree by myself.

But if my kids are living near us, I hope they'll invite me to join my grandchildren in selecting a tree.

The next generation needs to be indoctrinated.

<><><>

Find JPC Allen online:

***Website and blog: www.JPCAllenWrites.com***
***Facebook: https://www.facebook.com/JPCAllenWrites/***
***Instagram: https://www.instagram.com/jpcallenwrites/***
***Goodreads:***
***https://www.goodreads.com/author/show/18623122.J_P_C_Allen***

# Not This Year

## *By Sandra Merville Hart*

### Chapter 1

Ed Farmer usually walked to the parking lot with one of his coworkers, joking to unwind after a tough day at the machine shop. Not today. Devastated by news that the boss delivered that morning, he took his time at his locker, donning his blue winter coat that had weathered several seasons. He picked up his lunch box and empty Thermos and looked around. Everyone was gone. Good. He wasn't up for sympathizing with anyone about the company cutting their hours in January.

Looked like the new year of 1985 was going to be even worse than this year.

At least the company waited until after Thanksgiving to spread the bad news.

Clara wasn't going to be happy about the pay cut. Finances were already stretched to the breaking point, but his wife of nearly thirty years would stand beside him. Support him. She always did.

He trudged to his car, the weight of the world on his shoulders. They were barely making ends meet with him working fifty-five hours a week. How were they going to make it on forty?

Worry escalated to anger as he drove home from work in the late November darkness. Twinkling, colored lights from many homes reflected the Christmas spirit and foretold the coming holiday.

Gifts. Another expense they couldn't afford, especially now.

"Thanksgiving turkey leftovers still in the fridge," he muttered under his breath and then looked around. There was no one in the car on his way home from work, but he didn't want folks in other cars to see him talking and think him crazy.

Christmas decorations and store advertisements bombarded his senses as he approached a mall. Tapping on his brakes from extra traffic on the road did nothing to improve his mood.

A traffic light turned red. He slowed to a stop. Santa waved to him from outside the door of a store Clara favored, ringing a bell to call attention to a big black pot beside him. Ed grimaced and averted his eyes. Everyone had their hand out this time of year.

"Christmas is becoming too commercial," he said aloud.

Buying gifts wasn't what Christmas was all about anyway.

Why didn't the stores advertise that message? The answer brought another grimace. Not good for business.

Of course, Ed loved giving presents to his family as much as the next guy. A sigh came from the depths of his soul. He wasn't made of money.

What could be done?

Rubbing a hand across his furrowed brow, he drove one-handed away from city lights. Down darker streets.

There was one option.

He had always threatened not to buy any gifts for Christmas.

After paying the bills that screamed the loudest, his pay barely stretched to putting meat on the table. With credit card balances nearly at the limit, how was he to pay for gifts for his wife and four children? Not to mention his new son-in-law. His middle daughter, Laura, had married Ryan over the summer—they were both attending a Bible college in Missouri some 600 miles from her childhood home in Ohio and didn't have money to come in for the holidays. Though his youngest child, Katie, was a senior in high school, the other two worked full-time to put themselves through college. Brad, his oldest, still lived at home, though he was barely there except to eat and sleep. His job as assistant manager at a local store was a demanding one—along with two college classes per semester and an active social life. As long as he was in school, Ed wanted him to stay—it was the only help toward college expenses he was able to give. Alyssa had her own apartment, but she didn't make much at her office job. She came over a couple of nights a week for supper. He worried about her.

Not to mention Clara's parents. Frank and Pearl had lived with them over twenty years. They gave Clara a little toward rent, but their pension didn't cover their insurance and medical bills. The difference fell on Ed's shoulders. Though it went against the grain, he'd once asked for help with those insurance costs from one of Clara's siblings—the person most likely to step to the plate. One check for twenty-five dollars. That was all the money he received to pay for years of bills. A slap in the face would have been easier to take. He'd never asked for help again.

Not that he minded taking care of them. His own parents—gone now—had raised him to look after family. Yet those sacrifices had caused his own children to go without over the years.

Tension settled in his gut, hard as a stone. He banged the steering wheel with the heel of his hand—how could he stomach adding to the family's debt this Christmas with frivolous gifts?

He couldn't. Not this year. Something had to give.

The family had heard his warning for years. This year he'd follow through—there'd be no gifts under the tree. He clenched his jaw. It had to be.

## Chapter 2

Lights reflected against closed curtains when Ed pulled into the driveway of his country home. Clara always managed to make his humble ranch home nice and cozy. The sight of every room lit welcomed him as he parked outside what had once been the garage, renovated years ago to a bedroom for Brad.

A white Toyota nestled on the graveled area he'd created between the grass and the road. Good, Alyssa was here tonight. He missed her something fierce since she'd moved out last summer.

Frank and Pearl, Clara's parents, greeted him from their usual spots around the supper table.

Ed, his heart heavy, pasted on a smile. "Evening, folks." Tempting aromas wafted in from the kitchen. Fried chicken. His stomach growled.

Clara smiled up at him as she carried in a steaming platter of fried chicken. She set it on the table and then tilted her face for his kiss. "Hungry?"

"You bet." He leaned to kiss the petite woman who still made his heart beat faster with her sweet smile. "Everything okay here?"

"Just fine." She smiled. "Alyssa's mashing the potatoes. I set a place for Brad, but who knows if he'll be here for supper. Katie's on the phone—" She peered over Ed's shoulder into the living room. "Oh, good. She's off now."

"Hi, Dad."

Ed turned. Katie, brushing her long blonde hair behind her ear, reached to hug him. "There's my girl." He gave her a one-armed hug. "Did you have a good day?"

"Yeah." She followed him into the kitchen where Alyssa dished up creamy mashed potatoes into a large serving bowl, the purple swirled design disappearing more with each spoonful.

Setting his lunchbox on a counter, he put an arm around Alyssa. All his girls were petite like their mama. "You good, honey?"

"Just fine." Her brown hair, curly from a perm, brushed against his arm. "Glad not to have class tonight."

"Good to see you." The family's presence began to comfort him.

He sat at the head of the table with Clara on his right side. When Brad slid into his chair right before Katie asked the blessing, he smiled. Only two missing—Laura and Ryan. With everyone's crazy schedules, it wasn't too often that the rest of the family sat around the table together.

"Katie, would you ask the blessing?" Ed folded his hands.

The family plowed into the meal as soon as Katie finished praying. There was one piece of chicken per person with a wing left over. His appetite dwindled. Even fried chicken might become a luxury come January.

"Dad, can we put up the tree Sunday afternoon?" asked Katie. "I work all day Saturday."

Ed's stomach clenched. Best nip this one in the bud before anyone shopped for the holiday. "Do we need a tree if we're not buying presents?"

Clara's face blanched.

Ed reached for her cold hand. Her fingers closed around his, a question in her eyes. He should have warned her first.

"Not buying gifts?" asked Alyssa. "What are you talking about?"

"Christmas is getting too commercial to suit me." He gulped at the stunned looks around the table.

"You say that every year." Pearl believed in speaking her mind. "What's different now?"

He took a deep breath. "You may as well know. They're cutting our hours in January. Found out today."

Clara's hand jerked within his.

Rough news for her, too. "With the economy the way it is, we've got to cut expenses in this house. Gifts aren't what Christmas is all about anyway."

Clara's hand went limp. Then she pulled away from him, staring at her mashed potatoes as if she'd never seen the vegetable.

"That's the truth." Pearl raised her eyebrows. "How much are they cutting your hours?"

"Fifteen hours a week. I'll be on a forty-hour schedule."

"For how long?" Clara's brown eyes lost their luster.

"Don't know. We were supposed to get a large order last month—would have kept us all working overtime for a year. It didn't come." The weight of their financial burden descended on his shoulders. "We have small jobs. The company isn't in danger of closing." Though he worried about lay-offs. Best not mention that concern.

"I didn't know that." Alyssa's brown gaze bounced from him to her mom.

Ed stared at the chicken breast cooling on his plate."The CEO still expects the order to come through." He swallowed. "Might be February or March." Or later. No guarantees. "Should go back to working overtime when that happens."

Silence.

"You mean we can't buy gifts this year?" asked Katie.

"I mean that your mother and I won't be buying any gifts this year. You all should save your money, too." Ed speared a cold green bean and shoved it into his mouth.

"I still want to put up the tree." Katie raised a crestfallen gaze to her mom.

"That's fine." Clara's voice strengthened. "We will decorate for Christmas on Sunday."

The family's stunned silence bothered Ed, who was used to the conversation flying from one person to another.

Clara sipped her iced tea, avoiding his gaze.

Ed tried not to mind. After all, she had heard him complain in past years about the expense. His decision not to waste money on gifts shouldn't come as a shock. It was justified.

His determination grew. January would be tough enough without paying for Christmas presents.

## Chapter 3

Ed hauled a big box containing the family Christmas tree from the attic that Sunday. His heart wasn't in it—he put the silver branches into their slots only to please Clara.

"Sit down a few minutes." Without looking at him, Clara pointed to his blue recliner. "The girls can decorate the tree with me."

She was still angry with him for not talking with her first. They'd had a private discussion—he preferred not to call it an argument—the other night after everyone went to bed. He apologized, but his mind had been made up. He hadn't agreed to her coaxing for one small gift to everyone, knowing how easy it was for the cost to snowball out of control.

"Okay," he said now. Yep, Clara was hopping mad—and equally worried about the coming pay cuts.

Alyssa had brought Katie home from church. The girls tried to follow their mom's lead and treat this decorating party just like every other year. In fact, after lunch they'd strung some popcorn to add to the tree decorations, something they rarely did.

Ed sat back with his feet up. His exhausted body realized how tired it was and, before all the red tinsel was wrapped around the tree, he fell asleep.

<><><>

Ed continued to work ten-hour days and a five-hour shift on Saturday for the next two weeks. Mid-December and no news of the large order. Some of the guys he worked with actually looked forward to dropping to forty hours. They didn't need the money as much as the rest.

Ed had to agree about the exhaustion—the long hours were brutal. With his fifty-fourth birthday looming next month, he wasn't getting any younger.

But he was accustomed to hard work. Had worked hard all his life—an aching body at the end of the day was normal for him.

He entered an unusually quiet home that evening. Katie was working. Brad had class. Alyssa didn't stop by. After a subdued supper, Pearl and Clara cleaned the dishes. Frank watched television in his room.

Ed sat in his recliner, gazing at the silver tree. That empty tree skirt bothered him more than he cared to admit. Every year, he'd always asked Clara for her wish list and then taken one of his daughters to help him pick it out for her. Not buying his beautiful wife a gift bothered him more than anything else.

There should be a gift down there for her.

Rubbing lotion on her hands, Clara sat on the end of the couch closest to his recliner. "I'm done for the day." She leaned her head against the brown-cushioned couch with a long sigh. "Glad those dishes are done. I made up a plate for Katie and Brad."

"Good." He glanced at her. Exhaustion lined her face. "Just looking at the tree and relaxing a bit myself."

"We're out of milk."

"I've got enough cash on me for a gallon of milk. I'll go get some." He lowered the feet of the recliner.

"Thanks, but I want to talk to you first."

He raised his eyebrows at her serious tone. "What about?"

"Mama and Daddy gave me fifty dollars. They thought we could use our Christmas gift early."

He gave a low whistle. "Quite generous. More than they've ever given us."

"Yeah. They're not giving the kids anything this year so they could do a little more for us."

Taking anything away from his children didn't set well with Ed. "Wish they hadn't done that."

"It was their choice." Clara gazed at the empty tree skirt. "I want to use it to buy Katie a gift or two."

Sweat beaded on his forehead. "You know we can't afford—"

"I'm not asking you to spend any of your paycheck." Her face hardened. "This is the way I want to spend my Christmas gift from my parents. I can give you your portion of the check."

He stifled a sigh. They could use that money for something practical… like chip away at a mountain of debt.

"The older kids got presents every year. It was never much, but they got them." She crossed her arms, her hands tightening into fists. "Katie should have something to open on Christmas. I'll spend my portion on her. I don't know what you want to do."

"That amount would buy a couple of nice gifts for her." He

rubbed his chin. It'd be nice to see a gift or two under the tree. Clara wasn't the only one who wanted their youngest daughter to have a good Christmas. "We'll shop this weekend."

"Good." Her fingers relaxed yet her posture remained rigid. "There's something else."

Oh, boy. Ed straightened his shoulders. "Okay. Shoot."

"It's actually good news." She lifted her chin. "Brad says he'll double the amount of rent he gives us starting next month."

"No." The back of Ed's neck turned hot. "Out of the question."

"He wants to help."

Ed swiped his damp forehead. "He's paying for college. Providing him a place to live while he does that is the only help I can give him." Hard words to say. "You know that."

"We should accept his help."

"I ain't no blamed charity case." Ed jumped to his feet. "I'll go after the milk."

Arms folded, Clara stared silently at the tree as he shoved his arms into his winter coat and stalked outside.

The very idea. Brad needed that money to pay for college—else he'd be in his own apartment already. He might have to drop a class or two to help out his old man.

Not on Ed's watch.

As he handed over the last dollar in his wallet to the clerk, a heavy weight descended on his chest, making it difficult to breathe. Money had been in short supply his whole life. Why did it bother him so much now?

He cradled the milk to his chest and left the small grocery market in the dark. Maybe he was tired of seeing his family go without.

## Chapter 4

Christmas shopping with Clara on Saturday afternoon filled a void in Ed. He'd complained every year about the money spent on presents for the kids, only able to envision debts mounting. This shopping trip was different—they spent their Christmas gift on Katie.

Clara shopped at two stores in the mall, one near their home and another near his work, without purchasing anything.

"You're determined to get the best price, aren't you?" he teased. It wasn't a complaint, because he enjoyed the sparkle in his wife's eyes too much.

"We have to get the most bang for our buck." She smiled. "Let's go back to the mall. Sears has the best sales right now."

They stepped outside into freezing temperatures. Someone dressed as Santa rang a bell next to a big black pot.

Ed cringed. He liked giving to charities, especially the Salvation Army, but things were tight. Quickening his step, he averted his eyes.

Clara elbowed him.

He glanced at her.

Raising her eyebrows, she gave a slight nod toward Santa standing in the cold.

Sighing, he opened his wallet and extracted a dollar that wafted into the pot where coins and a few bills covered the bottom.

"God bless you." Santa smiled and rang the bell harder.

"And God bless you." Reaching for Ed's hand, Clara smiled at the stranger.

A smile touched Ed's lips as they crossed the parking lot toward his brown Dodge Dart. He squeezed Clara's hand, glad she'd forced him to open his wallet.

Giving back at Christmas caused the tension to ooze from his shoulders, even when that amount was small. Added to other gifts, dollars and quarters swelled to an amount that made a difference.

Clara knew that. He needed to remember it, too.

<><><>

Ed only shopped once. He and Clara so enjoyed being out together, alone, that it seemed like a date. He had hated to see their day end.

That shopping done, he expected to feel relieved about missing the frantic Christmas shopping crowds that Clara had dragged him to repeatedly in the past … truly his least favorite part of the season. But relief never came. Surprisingly, one shopping trip didn't satisfy him.

Why was he more upset this year than in previous years when they had far exceeded their shopping budget?

Not wanting to hear his coworkers' news about gifts they'd

purchased for their family, Ed didn't go to the employees' room to each lunch with the guys on the Friday before Christmas. He, who had always been able to share the joy of another's good fortune, protected himself from hearing it.

What was wrong with him? He knew Christmas meant more than the exchange of gifts. It was about a baby born 2,000 years ago, God's gift to the world.

Why did emptiness fill his soul?

At times, he almost regretted his decision to pay a few bills instead of buying gifts, but it was the right thing to do. No backing down now. Everyone was old enough to understand their money constraints.

He came home from a half day of work on Saturday and glanced at the tree. In addition to the two gifts they had wrapped for Katie under the tree, there were two more.

Clara brought a steaming bowl of vegetable soup in from the kitchen. "Hungry?" She set it in front of Frank, who sipped coffee at the dining table.

"You bet." He leaned for a kiss which she smilingly gave.

"Hi, Frank." Pearl carried a steaming bowl from the kitchen.

"Pearl. How's everyone?"

"Good." She smiled up at him. "Glad your work week is done?"

"Yeah." That always perked up his mood. "And we get off at three on Monday for the holiday. Even better. Where are the kids?"

"Katie's out with friends." Clara glanced at the empty couch with a sigh. "Brad's out. No telling when we'll see him since he mostly just sleeps here. Alyssa's busy this weekend but will be here Monday afternoon after work."

"She's working Christmas Eve?" He shrugged out of his coat and hung it in the coat closet beside the front door.

"Just like her dad."

Grimacing, he followed her to the kitchen where he washed his hands. "Didn't want her to take after me in that way. At this rate she'll be the richest girl in the graveyard."

"No, she won't." Shaking her head, Clara dipped a generous serving from a pot on the stove. "She doesn't make enough for that… and she's paying for college, remember?"

"How could I forget?" Ed pressed his lips together. Another

child he'd failed. "At least her company reimburses her for two of her classes every calendar year."

"And allows her to borrow a certain amount each year toward tuition." Clara carried a full bowl into the dining room. "Grab the crackers, will you?"

"Any news from Laura and Ryan?" He carried a pack of crackers to the table.

"Yes, they're leaving after church tomorrow to spend the holidays with his parents in Illinois." She sipped her sweet tea. "They sent the kids money for the trip."

Money he should have sent them to come to Ohio.

Clara asked the blessing on the food.

Wishing his budget had stretched to funding his son-in-law and daughter's trip, Ed tried to swallow the delicious soup past the lump in his throat.

## Chapter 5

On Monday morning, Ed listened for an announcement that the company had signed a contract for a large order in the coming year. In vain. His boss came by around ten and reminded him the machine shop would close down at three because it was Christmas Eve. He'd be paid for his normal eleven-hour shift.

He knew about closing early… being paid for eleven hours and working seven came as a welcome surprise. Christmas was a paid holiday—eight hours.

All the guys had brought in snacks for lunch. His contribution was buckeyes, peanut butter balls dipped in chocolate. He'd asked Alyssa to make them for him years ago when she was in high school. The guys loved them and asked for them each year. Katie had made them for the first time this year. He'd tried them at home last night and assured her that they tasted as delicious as Alyssa's.

Lunch was a festive meal with all the goodies. Pushing aside his dread of the coming evening, Ed laughed and joked with his friends. The company extended their lunch break to an hour.

He left the breakroom with a full stomach and a smile on his face.

The smile died as he pondered the next day and a half. Their tradition was to eat supper together on Christmas Eve and open one gift of their choosing. Then the kids went to church for the candlelight service.

Driving home, he clenched his jaw. Katie was the only one with gifts under the tree.

He longed to crawl into a hole.

Alyssa's car was already there when he arrived home. Katie was home. Brad was out.

The delicious aroma of chicken simmering in a pot wafted through the front door as he pushed it open. Chicken and dumplings tonight. The aroma piqued his appetite.

No one was in the room when Clara greeted him at the door with a kiss, smiling up at him.

"You seem happy." Studying her sparkling eyes, he hung his coat in the closet. "Are Laura and Ryan coming in after all?"

"They'll be here Thursday." Her dimples showed. "Ryan's parents gave them enough money to come here as well. They have to leave early Sunday," her smile dimmed, "but they're coming."

He held her close. "That's good news." His pride took a beating that he hadn't been the one to provide this treat for the couple still in college, but the joy on Clara's face comforted him.

"Not the only good news." She pulled away, her smile wavering.

"Oh, yeah?" His stomach clenched. Knowing her so well, he suspected she feared he wouldn't like the other "good news."

"Come with me to the basement." She tucked her hand inside his.

"You want me to carry up the laundry?" They used the unfinished basement as a laundry room and storage. The freezer was down there, too, along with canned goods.

"No, I'm not washing clothes today."

They descended the stairs. Ed scanned the large room for anything out of place, but only noticed a few clothes on the clothesline he'd strung almost the length of the basement. "What's up?"

"It's in here." She swung open the freezer door with a flourish.

Ed blinked. Then rubbed his eyes. Usually the only thing in the freezer was a loaf or two of bread. "What's all this?" He touched a white-papered butcher package on top of a pile packages just like it. Hard as a brick. A hand-written note marked it as stew beef.

"Meat?"

Clara's eyes glowed. "A side of beef."

Every shelf bulged with white-papered butcher packages.

"I don't understand." He gripped the freezer door. "Where did this come from?"

"Alyssa."

His head reeled. "What do you mean?" There had to be $300 worth of meat in this freezer—maybe more. Certainly more than had ever been there before. Tomorrow's turkey had been removed last week.

"This meat is her Christmas gift to the whole family this year."

"Where'd she get the money?" It was too much. Too expensive to accept.

"She used her whole Christmas bonus. I don't think it covered the entire cost, but she had a bit in her savings to make up the difference." She hugged a package. "Isn't it wonderful?"

"No." His breath hitched. Clara's smile should be reflected on his face too, but this was too great a gift. No one had ever given him so much. "I'll pay her back."

"You most certainly will not." Tossing back her shoulders, Clara drew herself up to her height of four-feet, ten inches. "This is a gift... a sacrificial gift that will feed us several months. You're going to be gracious and thank her for it."

His cheeks burned. "The sacrifice is too big." For Alyssa... or him? He brushed the thought aside.

"Allow your daughter to make that decision for herself."

"I can't." He rested his forehead on the open freezer door. "It cost too much."

"It's an amazing, practical gift. She's scared about what you'll say."

"You knew?"

Clara shook her head. "She called this morning. Said she'd bring a surprise for us. Asked me to clear the freezer shelves."

"Not much clearing to do."

"No."

He took one long look before closing the door. How was he to thank Alyssa past the shame that lodged in his throat? A man had his pride.

"Alyssa and Katie were hiding in Katie's room when you came in." The kitchen floor above them creaked. "No doubt she's waiting for you now. Be gracious."

He forced his legs to carry him across the concrete floor. Then he mounted the stairs as if a hangman's noose awaited him.

Alyssa stood beside the kitchen door. "Do you like it, Dad?" She wrung her hands.

"Yeah." He spoke in a monotone. "You did too much."

Color drained from her face. She turned and left the room.

Ed's shoulders hunched. He hadn't bought Alyssa one thing, yet she had used her whole bonus to purchase meat for his table. He'd used his to pay down on his credit card balances.

She'd have to return the meat. His heart shrank. What a mess he'd made of things.

**Chapter 6**

"Supper will be ready in about an hour. I'm making eggnog to go with the Christmas cookies Mama and I made this morning." Clara squeezed his hand and then turned toward the stove.

Pots and pans banged together as he left the kitchen.

*It's a Wonderful Life* was on television with his daughters and Pearl sitting around the living room, eyes on the screen.

*Jimmy Stewart doesn't know what he's talking about.* Ed sat at the empty dining table. Extracting a cigarette from a pack in his shirt pocket, he fumed over the gift in his freezer. It was too much. He'd have to talk to Alyssa about it. If, as he suspected, she used the family's butcher, maybe he could return it for her. Get her money back.

The meal of chicken and dumplings wasn't the festive occasion that Christmas Eve dinners usually were with everyone excited over opening gifts. Unable to decide how to handle a conversation about returning the meat with his daughter, Ed avoided looking at Alyssa.

"That's a practical gift you gave the family, Alyssa." Frank gave her one of his rare smiles. "I'm right proud of you."

"Me, too." Pearl patted Alyssa's arm. "What made you think of it?"

"I'd been trying to come up with a really practical gift for everyone." She shot a glance at her dad. "I was at the butcher's shop about a month ago and saw an advertisement for a side of beef. I thought about it for a while then went back and talked to him. He agreed to have it ready for me to pick up today."

"Since you couldn't wrap it." Katie smiled at her.

"No." Color stained her cheeks. "I could only keep the secret until today. I hope everyone likes it."

"I *love* it." Clara kicked Ed in the shins.

"Yeah," was all he could manage. He shoved a bite of dumpling into his mouth.

Alyssa gazed at her plate as silence fell.

Clara began talking about the cold weather. Ed could have kissed her for changing the subject. She understood his pride.

The long meal finally ended. Brad arrived when the dishes were done. He had already eaten.

"Since it's a tradition for us to open one gift on Christmas Eve," Clara's brown eyes pleaded with Ed, "let's have Katie open a gift tonight."

A fox in a hole couldn't feel more cornered. "Suits me," Ed agreed with a sinking heart. The time he dreaded most.

The family sat on the couch and cushioned chairs around the tree. Ed sat a little apart on his recliner.

"Can I choose the present I want to open tonight?" Gazing at the gifts, Katie pushed her blond hair behind her ears.

Clara nodded. "Of course."

Awkwardness descended on the family as Katie selected one of the gifts from her parents. Frank, Pearl, Alyssa, and Brad smiled, yet the atmosphere remained tense and strained.

Nothing was normal. Not this year.

Katie opened the gift slowly, stealing glances at everyone around the room. She smiled as she lifted a beautiful red sweater from the tissue.

Ed thought she'd look pretty wearing it, with her blond hair and brown eyes.

Brad picked up a small gift from beneath the tree. He offered it to Clara. "This is my gift to the whole family. You can open it tonight if you want."

Clara looked at Ed, who nodded. He couldn't remember a

more miserable Christmas.

Sliding her finger under each piece of tape prolonged the suspense. Ed knew how much she loved opening gifts. His heart ached that, for the first time in their marriage, he hadn't purchased her a present.

Clara stared at the contents.

"What is it, Mom?" asked Katie.

"Two checks for one hundred dollars each. One is for groceries. The other is for shopping." Blinking, Clara stared at the checks a long moment. She crossed the room to hug Brad.

"Those are both thoughtful gifts." Frank nodded his gray head in approval.

Ed clenched his hands. It was too much. Brad had to pay for college tuition. It was bad enough that he had to go on a part-time basis. At this rate, that degree would take years to receive.

"Yes, they are," said Pearl. "You kids did really good."

Ed scratched his head. Being on the receiving end of such large gifts stepped on his pride. It had never happened before… and he didn't know how to act. Maybe he'd best follow his wife's lead. Clara warned him to be gracious. "Thank you, son." His stilted words brought a relieved smile to his son's face. "We'll be using that next month."

Head bowed, Alyssa stared at her the wood floor.

"And you gave us a nice gift, too, Alyssa." Ed forced a smile past the tightness in his throat. He clamped his mouth shut on the objection that she spent too much. Her thoughtful, practical gift astounded him. Another kind of pride—the right kind—kindled in his soul.

"Glad you liked it, Dad." Her face relaxed into a genuine smile, her first one all day.

"Why don't you open the rest of your gifts, Katie?" asked Ed. "We'll sleep late in the morning."

Katie willingly opened the rest of her gifts. Brad and Alyssa had purchased her a gift as well. Ed moved to the couch to sit beside Clara. She tucked her hand inside his.

Later that evening, Ed stared at the emptiness underneath the Christmas tree. The kids went to the midnight service at church, and Frank and Pearl were in bed. Clara brought a glass of eggnog to Ed and joined him on the loveseat.

"We have great kids." She sipped her eggnog.

"Yes, we do." He put his arm around Clara. "They did too much."

"Can you blame them? They've watched you sacrifice for the ones you love all their lives."

He grunted. "Doesn't make it any easier to take."

She dimpled up at him. "Yes, you're used to being on the giving end."

"It's my preference."

"Mine, too." She sighed. "We're heading toward another rough patch, but we'll get through it."

What a strong woman he'd married. "You're the best wife a man could have."

"I am." She giggled. "And don't you forget it."

He kissed her, then snuggled her close. "I'm sorry I didn't buy you anything for Christmas."

"I'm sorry I didn't get you anything either."

Ed shook his head in wonder. "I thought that saving a little money at Christmas would make me feel better about the season. It didn't work. This is the worst Christmas of my life. I almost wish that everyone had complained about the lack of gifts."

"Instead they all rose to the occasion and gave practical gifts to us."

"Sacrificial gifts at that." He shook his head miserably. "I'll never do this to the family again—until I'm retired. May not have a choice then."

"Giving gifts is part of the joy of Christmas for me." Clara placed her empty glass on the end table and leaned on Ed's shoulder. He held her closer. "The gifts don't have to be costly. We can keep within a budget."

"I guess I needed an attitude adjustment."

Clara smiled at him.

He noticed she didn't argue about his bad attitude. "You know, I'm a lucky man."

"I do know." Her dimples appeared. "But why do you think you're lucky?"

"Because you said 'yes' to a bumbling fool all those years ago."

She giggled. "Not the description I'd use."

"I won't dig too deeply into what you *would* say." He laughed.

"But in all seriousness, God blessed me with a good woman. A wise woman."

"We'll get through this." Clara clasped his hand.

A load fell from Ed's shoulders. "I learned a lesson from my children this Christmas -- I'm a rich man." His fingers tightened around hers. "And I'd take that kind of wealth over money for the rest of my life."

# The Green Dress

*Every good and perfect gift is from above, coming down from the Father of the heavenly lights, who does not change like shifting shadows.* **James 1:17**

I stared at the red package under the tree with my name on it. Not that I could read it from my position between my siblings on the floor, but I knew which one was mine moments after my parents arranged the gifts under the tree earlier in the week. Santa had left a few toys for my brother, two sisters, and me during the night. Gifts under the Christmas tree were always something we needed, usually clothes.

Not that I minded receiving a pair of jeans, a dress, or a sweater for Christmas. Back-to-school shopping was the greatest source of new clothes for us and something I looked forward to every year. One birthday gift was usually a book or a puzzle or something for school. The only other opportunity for new garments was Christmas. My wardrobe had enough outfits for a different set each weekday. With two younger sisters, there was no chance for hand-me-downs. My hopes soared to add one more choice to the mix.

I glanced at a stack of new socks laying on top of underclothes…gifts I appreciated, but they didn't excite me.

Laura, my sister, tore open her last package. "Oh, pretty!" She held a peach dress with thin white, black, and peach stripes on the bodice and short sleeves up to her shoulders.

"Let me see it." My grandmother smiled as her hands trailed over the fabric. "I like it." She gave it back to Laura, who brought it to me.

"Do you like it?" Her green eyes widened.

"Sure." I knew my opinion mattered to her. "You'll look nice in it."

"Hope it fits." She smiled and ran to our bedroom to try it on.

Mama pointed at the red package. "You've got one more gift, Sandy."

"No time like the present." Daddy grinned. He enjoyed giving gifts more than anyone I knew, and Christmas was his favorite time of the year.

Anticipation rose up inside me. Laura's dress was pretty. Maybe mine would be just as nice. I dove under the tree for my last gift and tore it open.

What was this? My big present was a green dress? With dwindling enthusiasm, I held up it up for a better look. Sure enough, the bodice was the color of grass after a soaking rain. The A-line skirt was white with diagonal green stripes.

Nothing in my wardrobe was green … for good reason. My favorite colors were pink, blue, purple, peach, red—not green.

This was my ninth Christmas. I knew the drill. Money was always tight, but Mama would allow me to exchange the gift if it didn't fit or I didn't like it. Not wanting to hurt their feelings, I planned to try it on and say it didn't fit. We'd exchange it for something I liked, no questions asked.

"So how do you like your gift?" Daddy studied my expression. A bit of pride shone from his green eyes. "I usually leave choosing clothes for you kids to your mama. This time, when I saw that dress, I knew it would look pretty on my little Sandy."

My head jerked back as I looked up. Daddy *never* shopped for our outfits. "It's green, your favorite color."

"It is." His smile lit his face. "I can't wait to see it on you."

I looked at Mama, who smiled sadly at me. She'd noticed my disappointment with the gift.

"Why don't you try it on?" She glanced at my dad. "If it doesn't fit, we'll return it for something else."

"It fits!" Laura dashed into the living room. "I get to keep it."

That peach shade complimented her curly brown hair. It looked beautiful on her. Disappointment sank deeper. Why wasn't my new dress as pretty as hers?

While my parents and grandparents gushed over Laura's appearance, I carried my big present to our bedroom. My only hope now was that it didn't fit.

With my luck, it probably would fit just fine.

I slipped the soft fabric over my head and zipped up the back.

My heart sank. A perfect fit. Almost like it was made for me.

I couldn't express my disappointment in the dress—that would hurt my dad's feelings. He'd lack the courage to select future gifts. He'd apologize to my mom for bungling their Christmas shopping.

On the other hand, it was a sacrifice to wear something I didn't like because there'd be no new clothes until school started next fall.

Both of these dismal prospects depressed me. Only one was in my power to mend.

I plastered on a smile and sashayed into the living room like I was a model.

"Wow!" My dad sat straight up. "It fits you." He hugged my mom, who sat beside him on the couch. "Honey, look at that. Your daughter looks pretty in the dress I picked, just like I told you. Thanks for trusting me on this one. She ought to be able to wear it a couple of years anyway."

His joy bolstered my plastered-on smile. I liked making my dad happy. And the dress wasn't half bad, really. At least, that's what I tried to convince myself.

I wore my new dress on the first day back from Christmas vacation. Some of my friends noticed and complimented me on it. After that, I wore it often to please my dad.

"Sandy's wearing that pretty green dress again," I'd hear him say to my mom. "I did a good job picking it out. She loves it."

Before long I noticed that my attitude about the dress had changed. It wasn't so bad after all. No longer did I have to force myself to don it. In fact, I grew to love the comfortable dress that fit like it was made for me.

Perhaps it was.

Long into my adult years, I remember sitting at the table after a delicious, satisfying meal prepared by my mom, and listening to stories about my dad's childhood pour from the gifted storyteller. One story he often told was about the time he picked out a Christmas gift for me. His face softened to recall how much it pleased him each time I wore it. He spoke of how he could still see me in it in his mind's eye.

My memories traveled back through the years. I dismissed that old disappointment as if it were dirt to be swept into a dustpan and discarded. What I remembered was his joy in giving it to me. My eyes misted. "I loved that dress." I meant every word. He'd chosen it especially for me. That made it special.

He tilted his head at me. "I did good?"

Recalling all his sacrifices through the many lean years to take care of his family, I covered his workworn, callused hand with mine. "You did very good." I smiled, looking into eyes filled with warmth, love, and a color that had become one of my favorites…green.

<><><>

Find Sandra Merville Hart online:

***Sandra's blog, https://sandramervillehart.wordpress.com/.***
***Facebook: https://www.facebook.com/sandra.m.hart.7***
***Twitter: https://twitter.com/Sandra_M_Hart***
***Pinterest: http://www.pinterest.com/sandramhart7/***
***Amazon Author Page: https://www.amazon.com/Sandra-Merville-Hart/e/B00OBSJ3PU/***

# Return to Callidora

### *By Laurie Lucking*

**Chapter 1**
(Eveline)

*He's not coming.*

I leaned my forearms against the window ledge, lamenting the droves of fluffy, drifting snowflakes. Only the fiery orange scales of an enormous tail rounding the corner of my tower marred the endless white scene below. Aodhan, the dragon placed here as my guardian, must've found a jackrabbit to chase.

I shut my eyes and turned away, clamping down my hope before it could rise in my chest like a phoenix. Certain to burn me in the end.

He usually arrived close to the noon hour, and it was nearly dusk.

I'd always looked forward to Ryker's annual visits as a break from the monotony of my tutor and nursemaid. But this year, after a full twelve months of complete solitude...

I swiped a hand across my eyes. *No sense crying, Eveline. What if your knight in shining armor chose to arrive at this moment, only to find you with swollen, red eyes?* Straightening, I marched toward the kitchen. Christmas Eve or not, I could always find more work to do.

After donning an apron, I removed my grinder from the shelf and poured in a measure of wheat. My throat tightened as I replaced the sack on the countertop. Too light. Without Ryker's delivery of my usual supplies, it'd be empty by week's end.

*No.* I couldn't think like that. Bread wasn't a necessity of life. My teeth clenched as tightly as my hands as I turned the crank around. Did I have the wrong date? I sped up my work. As soon as the dough was ready, I'd go to my bedroom and check.

I let my mind wander as I added water and yeast and kneaded the resulting dough. Perhaps Ryker delayed his departure because of the snow and would arrive over the next few days. But what if something happened to him? Or worse. What if something happened to the entire kingdom of Callidora?

My hands stilled. I was so isolated that my homeland could be destroyed or overtaken without me even knowing it. Kirra, the sorceress who'd sworn vengeance against me in my childhood when my parents refused to make me her apprentice, couldn't touch me while I was under a dragon's protection—apparently their innate powers dampened any attempts at artificial human magic in their presence. But what if she went after my family instead?

Shuddering, I folded the dough one last time, then laid a cloth on top. After peeking in on my garden to pluck a peapod, I wound my way up the steep, circular staircase that cut through the center of my tower. The structure's small footprint ensured Aodhan never strayed far from the sole entrance at the front. Instead, its size came from rising high into the air, with one room on each of its many landings.

Halfway to my bedroom on the highest floor, an odd noise mingled with my echoing footsteps. As though Aodhan had been preparing to roar but was cut off. I raced to the nearest window. *Ryker*!

I dashed back down, around and around until dizziness made my head swim. Coming to a sudden halt at the bottom, I clutched the rail until my vision cleared. I ran forward and heaved the door open. The man before me bore a closer resemblance to a tall, gangly snowman than my friend, but I'd recognize that freckled nose anywhere.

"You're here!" I threw my arms around him, pressing my cheek into the thick fabric surrounding his shoulders. "I thought you'd never come."

He huffed. Melting snow dampened the front of my dress, but I squeezed harder.

I felt more than heard his chuckle as his stiff arms enclosed my back.

"Of course I came. And I'm happy to see you too, Ev." He drew back just as Aodhan let out a snort.

"Oh, come in, quick." I backed up, allowing him to lead his horse through the narrow doorframe. "Aodhan doesn't stay asleep for long, does he?"

He shook snowflakes from the light-brown strands of hair

clinging to his forehead. "You know I have to wake him again the moment we're past. Can't leave an opening for Kirra, now can we?

"I suppose not. But your poor horse looks terrified." I stroked the animal's neck and unstrapped one of the many saddlebags.

"Probably more cold than anything. Isn't that right, Mushroom?" Ryker ran a hand over the horse's mane before removing a bag from the other side.

"Mushroom?"

He shrugged. "I didn't name him. I just take whatever the stable hands offer."

I released the last saddlebag with a grunt, easing it to the floor. My supplies ought to be well-stocked for the coming year. I prayed I wouldn't need them much longer than that.

"Let's get him settled."

Ryker slung several bags over his shoulder. "Lead the way."

I took off down the corridor to a large, plain room just off the entrance that had been supplied with hay, thick blankets, and food and water troughs. Footsteps and hoof clicks trailed behind me.

"How did you convince a horse through this blizzard? *Mushroom* doesn't seem too happy about it."

"Doesn't only work on dragons, you know." Ryker waved his long, thin pipe before tucking it back beneath his cloak. "I had him in a trance for most of the ride. He didn't get grumpy until I had to switch over to putting Aodhan to sleep."

Ryker's musical talent had a profound effect on animals. By gauging their size, mood, and who knew what else, he could secure the obedience of the most feral beasts with a simple tune. Upon discovering that Ryker could cause Aodhan to sleep or wake simply by playing his pipe, my parents had immediately hired him as my exclusive messenger. He came once every year, the day before Christmas.

"Thank you for coming in this dreadful storm. Even if your horse got to be in a trance, you had to endure it."

"I'd never let you down, no matter the weather."

I glanced to him, and the corners of his mouth tipped up.

Once we had Mushroom situated, Ryker and I each donned several saddlebags and headed for the kitchen. I lowered my bags to the floor and began rifling through.

"Let's get you something to eat. I have bread, and my

strawberry preserves turned out well this year. Hopefully Cook sent the usual butter and cheese. Oh, and—"

"Ev, slow down." Ryker tugged at my arm. "I'll last a few more minutes, I promise."

I straightened. "But your journey must've been miserable, in all that snow."

"I'm fine." He stepped closer. "You're the one I'm concerned about. How are you?"

"Same as ever, as you can see." I tried to keep my smile steady.

He blew out a small chuckle. "Not quite the same. Your hair is longer. And your eyes..."

I squirmed under his scrutiny.

"A little wiser, perhaps." His grin faded. "But you've been well? Plenty to eat and drink? No illnesses? No signs of Kirra?"

"Yes. The well hasn't run dry, my garden still grows, and illness is rare when one stays indoors at all times with no other human contact."

He winced and shifted his feet.

"As for Kirra, to my knowledge she hasn't come anywhere near. Though I'd hardly know what to look for if she had."

"Aodhan seems as sharp as ever, so you should be safe."

I nodded. "Now, about that meal. Do you like tomatoes? I can't remember."

"Tomatoes sound wonderful."

Soon I had eggs and meat frying over a fire and a plate laden with vegetables, bread, and cheese set before Ryker.

"There's been quite a bit of talk about you lately, you know." He swallowed, keeping his eyes fixed on his plate.

"Me?" I prodded a sizzling egg. "I'm surprised anyone remembers I exist."

"No one's forgotten about you—you're practically legend in Callidora." He cleared his throat. "It's no secret you recently came of age."

"What does that matter? I could hardly host a ball to celebrate." I transferred the cooked food onto another platter and approached the table.

Ryker sighed. "Now that you're eighteen, I think many would-be rescuers are just waiting until the snow clears."

"Really?" The plate clattered onto the table. "I don't

understand why anyone would bother. None of them have even met me."

"Your beauty is highly reputed throughout the kingdom."

"Is it?" My heart flailed, but the surge of vanity didn't last. "But what if I don't live up to my reputation? What if someone slays the dragon and then takes one look at me and heads back out the door?"

He coughed, red tingeing his ears. "Not possible."

"I might be a disappointment."

"You won't."

I lowered onto a chair and popped a cube of venison into my mouth. "My life will change so suddenly, all in one moment."

"A change for the better." Ryker reached across the table for my hand. "You deserve to be surrounded by people who love you, wearing fancy gowns and attending banquets and dancing at balls." He squeezed my fingers, then drew his arm back. "Not serving a meal to the poor musician you're stuck with for company."

I threw a napkin at him. "You know I'm thrilled to have your company."

"Only because you have no other options." He tossed the napkin back with a flourish.

After he scraped the last bite from his plate, he rose and stretched. "I hope poor Mushroom's warmed up a bit. We'd best be on our way."

"What?" I halted on my way to the wash basin. "You just got here."

His breath fluttered the hair on his forehead. "I know, but getting back won't be any easier than the trip here. The daylight's already gone."

"But you always stay for Christmas."

"That was when your tutor was still here." He rubbed the back of his neck. "Your parents wouldn't like it."

"They never need to find out. I have your usual room prepared." I grasped his arm. "Please? You can't know what it's like, being left alone for an entire year. When Frances went with you last time, I thought I was happy to see her go. Now I'd give anything for her lectures and scolding. To have someone to talk to."

"Oh, Eveline. I know it's been hard." He placed a warm hand

on my back. "All right, I'll stay. But just for one night."

I clapped. "Thank you! What fun we'll have. With all the new supplies, I can cook something special." My heart drooped. "Even that doesn't seem like much, though. I wish you could stay longer."

"I definitely couldn't agree to that." He raised an eyebrow at my pout. "Just think how it would look to your rescuer to find a man already here."

"He wouldn't have anything to worry about from *you*."

His jaw tightened. "Because I'm so very insignificant?"

Ugh, men and their pride. "No, Ry, that's not what I meant." I stepped closer. "I just know you would never...take advantage of being alone with me."

"Of course I wouldn't." His cheeks turned pink. "But he wouldn't know that."

"True. I can't afford to send my knight into a jealous rage the moment he walks through the door." I retreated to the wash basin. "But I still don't see why my tutor had to be sent away."

"Apparently you were done with your studies."

I blew out a breath. "You know what I mean. Couldn't I at least have a maid?"

"And what would your brave knight do with the extra companion when he rescues you?" He smirked. "Leave her here? Heft her up onto his horse behind the two of you? Bring an extra mount?"

"Oh, you're impossible." I flung a cascade of droplets toward him.

He ducked. "Just thinking it through the way I'm sure your parents did. I doubt they would've forced you into solitude if they could've devised a good alternative."

"Maybe." My sense of mischief faded. "I sometimes feel like they just took the easiest path. Locking me away until I can be someone else's problem."

"Ev." Ryker came to my side and squeezed my shoulder. "Your parents love you. It shows in their faces every year as they fret over whether they've packed enough supplies. I'm not sure they chose the best path when dealing with Kirra, but I believe they tried to do what they thought was right."

"Thanks. What would I do without you, Ry?"

"Be a whole lot drier." He splashed water into my face, and I shrieked.

<><><>

Ryker slumped beside me on the settee in my sitting room. Moisture curled the ends of his hair. "Don't let me interrupt you."

I folded up the letter from my sister I'd been reading and placed it back into its envelope. "Nonsense. I'll have plenty of time to read these later."

He angled toward me, lounging against the overstuffed cushion. "What's the news from your family?"

"Nothing of much import. Vanessa hates her Dalonese lessons, Edmond finally gets to learn fencing. My parents seem fine."

Ryker quirked a brow.

Oranges and blues twirled within the hearth. "You can only fit so much into one annual letter. I barely know them anymore."

"After your triumphant return to the palace, you'll have plenty of opportunities to make up for lost time."

"I suppose." I fiddled with the lace trim on my gown. Ryker felt more like a brother now than any of my siblings by blood. I'd barely recognize them when—if—I finally made it home.

A snort from outside punctured the silence. I ran to the window, my pulse pounding like a stampede. Aodhan landed in a spray of snow. His long jaws clenched a limp hawk.

Ryker peered over me. "Everything all right?"

"Yes." I leaned against the window frame. "Just Aodhan hunting."

He chewed his lower lip. "It seems cruel the poor creature's meant to die in the end. After protecting you all this time."

"I know." I returned to my spot on the settee, tilting my head back. "I've grown rather fond of him, and it isn't fair he has to be killed by my new protector simply to prove a point. They could just as easily have a tournament. If the goal is to get the strongest, bravest, most skilled knight to be my husband, that would serve the purpose just as well."

Ry stiffened before returning to my side. "Is that the goal, though?"

"Of course. Who else could they want to save me?"

He nudged me, directing my attention to a tapestry on the wall. It depicted the Son as a babe in his cradle in the forefront, a man hanging on a cross in the background. "Courage comes in many forms, after all."

My gaze lingered on the scene. A helpless baby, grown into a man who never donned a suit of armor. Never once raised a sword. And yet saved all of humankind.

"I suppose it does."

## Chapter 2
*(Ryker)*

I settled further under my covers and savored one last moment of luxurious rest. My thoughts drifted to Eveline's sweet kiss on my cheek the evening before. I was such a fool, but at the moment I couldn't quite make myself care.

With one final yawn, I rolled out of bed and changed into my riding clothes. I took the stairs two at a time, in circle after circle. The scent of bacon wafted from the kitchen.

"Merry Christmas!" Eveline's warm smile widened mine.

"Merry Christmas." I joined her by the fire. "This smells wonderful, but you shouldn't be making this much effort just for me."

"Yes, I should. I can't tell you how excited I am to have someone to spend the holiday with." She perched her hand on her hip. "Besides, I'm rather proud that I have more domestic skills than any princess in history."

"You certainly do." I rummaged through cupboards until I had enough plates and silverware to set the table.

No trace of her somber mood from the night before darkened Eveline's face as she chatted through breakfast. She seemed determined to expel every bit of conversation she'd missed over the past year. I studied the yellow flecks in her blue-green eyes, the way her nose crinkled when she laughed, and the elegance of her hand gestures, only catching a portion of her words. But my intent gaze and occasional nods gave her sufficient assurance I was paying attention.

Her fork clattered against her empty plate. "All right, I can't wait any longer. Are you ready for your present?"

"If you insist." I shoveled one last bite into my mouth before pushing my chair back.

She led me to her sitting room, which now had gifts strewn about the floor.

"I took out the ones from my family, too." She practically skipped across the rug. "Now sit."

I obeyed. She rifled through the gifts and lifted a large, flat rectangle draped in a white cloth.

"Hmm, I think you picked the wrong one." I narrowed my eyes. "That doesn't look like my usual sweater or scarf."

Her cheeks reddened. "No, you've seen the last of my misshapen knitting projects."

"No matter their shape, I'm honored to have the rare distinction of hand-knitted gifts from the princess."

Her melodious laugh warmed the room. "Even a scarf that's several inches wider on one side than the other?"

"That's my favorite."

Shaking her head, she sat at my side. "Well, now that Frances is no longer here to force me to practice my knitting, I've returned to the kind of needlework I prefer." She laid the gift across my lap. "Merry Christmas, Ryker."

I didn't dare meet her eyes. Who knew what idiocy I might fall into with her perched so close, the moment so intimate? I lifted the thin fabric and puffed out a breath. With vibrant colors and minute precision, she'd stitched her tower, with Aodhan prowling near the mahogany frame. At the entrance stood a girl in a rose-colored dress with long, golden hair greeting a tall, slim boy with a blue knit cap.

"Ev, it's remarkable."

"I wanted something for you to remember me by."

I nearly dropped the embroidery. "What do you mean by that?"

"As you pointed out last night, I'm of age now. Someone might come and rescue me, and even if they don't...a lot can happen in a year." She traced the edging of her sleeve. "You may get married and start a family, and your wife might not want you making this dangerous trek—"

"Nothing could stop me from making this trip, except you no longer being here. Not even a protective wife." I winced at the ludicrous idea. Eveline took up so much of my heart, there wasn't room for anyone who might actually consider marrying me.

She squeezed my wrist. "I appreciate that. But you deserve to find happiness too, Ry."

"This does make me happy." I studied the needlework once more before leaning the frame against the side of the couch. "Are you ready for your present?"

Her bouncing legs undermined her attempt at a stern look. "Ryker Trilesse, for the last time, you do not need to get me any presents. Making this journey every year is plenty."

"Your lectures are at least getting shorter." I reached inside my jacket and removed a long, thin package, cursing the tremble in my fingers. "Merry Christmas, Ev."

She accepted the gift, untying the twine and setting it gently aside. Her eyes widened as she unrolled the paper. "You can't give me your pipe! You need it to—"

"I didn't. I made another just like it." I pulled out my instrument and held it next to hers. "I thought you might appreciate a new hobby. If you like, I can teach you a bit today."

"Yes, please. Though I won't sound anything like you." She stroked a finger across the wood's jagged grain.

"Maybe someday you will."

Her giggle always made my chest tighten. "I love it, thank you." She circled her arms around my neck, tucking her head against my chest.

I held her close, inhaling her lilac scent. I might've run out and tried my luck with the dragon then and there, if it meant I'd stand a chance of marrying this girl. But my scrawny frame and low birth were nothing like the armored knight Eveline's parents had in mind. That she herself dreamed of. Squaring my jaw, I drew back. "Why don't you open the gifts from your family, then I can give you the lesson I promised. Mushroom and I should head out after lunch."

"Of course. But if you don't have time to teach me, I understand."

"I'll make time."

She walked to the pile of remaining gifts, glancing back to give me one of her heart-stopping smiles.

If that knight didn't show up soon, I was in serious trouble.

<><><>

Lunch was a more solemn affair, with my departure looming

over us. I tried to finagle some stew into my knotted stomach—I'd need it for the journey ahead.

After I shoved my spare clothes and a few provisions into my sack, I headed down the stairs. A clench in my chest told me it would be for the last time. I found Eveline with Mushroom, murmuring softly.

"I was giving him some encouragement for the trip home. At least the snow's let up, and he won't have all those heavy supplies to carry."

"We'll be fine." I squeezed her hand. "And so will you."

She nodded, her lips pressed into a tight line. We filed down the hall to the door, cheery as a funeral procession. Eveline reached for the door handle, but I stopped her.

"You'd better stay inside. I can't risk having you out there when I put Aodhan to sleep."

"I know." Red rimmed her eyes. "It's just hard to see you go."

"Believe me, I wish I didn't have to." I wrapped my arms around her, burying my face in her soft hair. "Someone will come for you soon, I'm sure of it." I tried to make the words comforting rather than bitter.

"I hope so." She leaned back. "If you're right, once I'm married and back in the kingdom, I'll make sure to visit you."

I wrestled a smile into place. "I'd like that."

Her face lingered only inches from mine, so open and affectionate. So achingly beautiful. Before I could stop myself, I pressed my lips to hers. Warm and soft as they parted, just like I'd...

*What was I doing?*

I stepped back and sucked in a breath. She gaped at me, her cheeks flushing. I had to make my escape quick before the moment became any more awkward.

Taking her hand, I kissed her fingers. "Goodbye, Princess." I fumbled for Mushroom's reins, then led him out the door.

"Good—goodbye." She continued to stare.

Cursing the heat searing my cheeks, I eased the door shut. I sure knew how to make an exit.

Mushroom stomped and brayed at my side. I patted his neck. "Sorry, boy. You're right, I can't forget the dragon." Aodhan swiped his wing at a passing night jay. More playing than hunting. I slid my pipe from its long, thin pocket. Leaving Mushroom in the shadow of the tower, I stepped forward and breathed a tune through the slender instrument. By the second stanza, the beast's large head swayed from side to side, then slowly curled onto its back.

"Good Aodhan." I ran a hand along his shiny scales as I returned to fetch Mushroom. Such a magnificent creature. Was it wrong to hope he bested the knights intent on slaying him?

Once we had several horse-lengths' clearance from the dragon, I hopped onto Mushroom's back. My fingers flew across the holes on my pipe, playing a lively tune. Soon Aodhan's head tipped up, his neck stretching high.

"That's our cue, boy." I dug my heel into Mushroom's side, and he galloped forward. "Guard her well, Aodhan." I longed to glance back at the tower for one last look at Eveline. But I'd botched my farewell enough already. Better to leave with feigned confidence, as though kissing her was a natural move for someone in my position.

Not the most idiotic thing I'd ever done.

I let the piercing wind numb my mind until nothing remained but my tense posture on Mushroom's back, my tight grip on the reins. Snow covered the ground in a heavy blanket, drifting to half a horse-length in places. I reluctantly slowed Mushroom to a walk.

A cry rent the air, followed by a low moan. What in the kingdom? Mushroom jerked and skittered to the side. I whispered into his ears as we turned in a full circle. "Good boy, steady now. Nothing to be afraid of." But my own heart drummed in my chest. What could—?

Another roar, decidedly animal-like. The only creature in the vicinity that could make that kind of sound was...Aodhan.

I pivoted Mushroom back toward the tower. After cantering for a few minutes, we slowed our approach. Groans continued to emanate from that direction, but quieter now. Less urgent. At the edge of the tree cover, I secured Mushroom's reins around a trunk. "Stay here, boy. I'll be back for you."

Ahead, all was quiet. Too quiet. Aodhan's massive form lay in a heap, motionless. I crept around, searching for signs of movement. Narrowing my radius, I eased closer, one hand on my pipe in case the dragon stirred. I *had* woken him again, hadn't I? I strained to see more of his massive body, something that might…

A low voice sounded from the direction of the tower. I ducked behind the dragon's tail, then peered out. A large man in a full suit of armor led a sturdy black steed near the entrance. He pivoted and held his sword aloft—the gilded handle reflecting the sunlight, the long, sharp edge coated in deep crimson.

## Chapter 3
*(Eveline)*

I wandered the tower, flitting from room to room. I should've put my gifts away or organized the storeroom. But Ryker's absence left a void no activity could fill. And that kiss… My fingers hovered over my lips. What had he meant by it? Perhaps it was merely a friendly gesture.

But then why had I felt so overcome by a desire to kiss him back?

I drifted to a window. No sign of him. I wandered away, stroking the tightly woven threads of a tapestry depicting an armor-clad knight raising his shield against the flames bursting from a dragon's mouth.

A roar brought me hurrying back to the window ledge. A tall, broad figure, encased in dark armor that glittered like onyx, swung his sword at the dragon, deflecting attempted blows from the beast's front legs. His horse, black as a starless night, stood firm beneath him. I gasped and stepped back. A knight had come for me? On *Christmas*? I tried to summon excitement, but nervousness came in its stead, edged with a hint of guilt.

My mind still lingered on Ryker.

I peered back out the window. The knight stood on top of Aodhan. The dragon seemed to be straining, as though wanting to beat his wings, but they didn't rise. The knight dodged a spray of fire, then lifted his sword.

Closing my eyes, I turned away. This was how it was supposed to end, but I couldn't watch the poor creature being butchered. Aodhan gave an agonized cry, then a low moan. I swiped at the tears welling in my eyes. My rescuer would hardly feel welcome if he found me crying over the dragon he'd slain.

But how should he find me, then? Panic surged through me.

I'd dreamed of this moment for so long, but always in general terms. Never the specifics.

Straightening the square neckline of my dress, I perched on the edge of my seat near the fireplace. Should I look more comfortable? I lounged back. *This was silly*. Rather than strike an absurd pose, I may as well meet him at the door. I could hardly pretend I hadn't noticed the skirmish taking place outside.

I wound down the staircase, tripping multiple times on my skirt. Goodness, my nerves had me in a state. I pulled my shoulders back, ran my hands over my hair, and raised my chin. Despite my sheltered upbringing, I was a princess, after all.

Easing the door open, I peeked through. Aodhan's head lolled, his body otherwise still. I swallowed against the tightness choking my throat. *Rest in peace, my fierce protector*. I angled the door wider. The knight hovered near the wall of the tower, his steed dancing at his side as he wiped dark blood from his sword.

With a helmet covering his face, it was impossible to read his expression. Or to tell whether he was handsome. He barely seemed winded from his confrontation with the dragon.

I let the door close behind me and strode forward.

The knight glanced up and straightened. "Princess! I thought I'd clean up a bit before presenting myself to you. But no doubt you heard the ruckus and came to investigate." He sheathed his sword and removed his helmet.

My heart skipped a beat. Possibly several. His blond hair curled at the ends just above his ears, his eyes a deep amber. A bit of scruff peeked out from his strong jawline.

"Oh. Yes. That is, I did hear something." I ended with a nervous giggle.

If I kept this up, he'd soon be convinced I was a half-wit.

He extended his hand. "Allow me to introduce myself. Sir Batair at your service, my lady. Though, of course, *you* may omit the Sir."

My hand looked like a child's in his firm grip. "It's a pleasure to meet you, Batair. I'm Princess Eveline. But you probably knew that already." My breathless laugh halted in my throat when he raised my hand to kiss it.

"The pleasure is all mine." His fingers stroked across my palm before releasing me, sending tingles up my arm. "Your beauty is acclaimed throughout the land, yet I was not prepared for such loveliness."

Heat invaded my neck, spreading to my face. "Thank you. You are really too kind."

"I speak only the truth."

Now what? All those years with a tutor and governess, and no one prepared me for how to properly receive my rescuer. "Would you like to come inside? You must be famished, and we can feed and water your horse, as well."

"We would like that very much. Thank you." He made a clicking sound to his horse, who trotted up beside us, skittering past the dragon's limp tail. "We'll follow your lead."

<><><>

*(Ryker)*

Edging along Aodhan's side, I made my way to a more secluded hiding place. Eveline emerged from the door, her shy demeanor only adding to her allure. I slowed my crawl, my heart sinking lower than the surrounding tree boughs heavy with snow. Less than an hour ago I'd held her in my arms, pressed my lips to hers. And now…

Soon they disappeared into the tower. If only I could follow. Eveline kept a dagger on her person at all times, but she wouldn't stand a chance against the knight if he intended to harm her. I rose cautiously, surveying the dragon once more. There must be—

I choked back a cry. Blood oozed from a large slit on his back just above his ribcage. I circled the area again, searching for signs of a struggle. How had he defeated the dragon so easily? I'd always assumed the old boy would put up quite a fight when the time came. A gleam caught my eye. I gingerly stepped over the beast's tail to get a closer look at its wing.

The blade of a knife protruded from the thin membrane, pinning it to the ground.

*He cheated*! The scoundrel must've snuck in and pinned the dragon's wings to the ground before it'd fully woken up.

I leaned against Aodhan's warm scales. A shuddering rise and fall pressed against my back. "Aodhan?" I couldn't raise my voice above a whisper. Another slight expansion of his chest. "You're breathing!" I jogged up beside his neck. A burgundy stream continued to ooze from his wound, pooling beneath him.

"Hang in there, I'll try to help."

I glanced back to the tower. No movement. Taking a deep breath, I sprinted to the nearest tree cover, then maneuvered to where Mushroom waited, stamping his hooves. "Patience, now. We have plenty of riding ahead of us." I gave him a pat before untying my pack from his saddle. Clutching my bag under one arm, I raced back to the dragon. I crouched beside him and dug out a length of fishing line. Further rummaging produced the thick needle I kept handy for shoe repairs. It would have to be enough.

I straightened, then extended to my toes to view the injury. I'd never reach well enough from this vantage point. Throwing an arm over his neck, I heaved myself up, using his scales as awkward footholds. The smell of raw flesh assaulted my nostrils. A layer of grayish tissue gaped open beneath the creature's vibrant scales. The stitches would have to go there. It took several attempts for my shaky hands to thread the fish line through the needle. Gulping, I pierced the sharp end through the tissue at the far edge of the wound. A hissing sound drew my gaze to Aodhan's head. One eye squinted open.

"Just me, no need to panic." I fumbled for my pipe—the next best thing to anesthetic. After a minute of soothing melody, his eye drifted shut again. "Good boy."

I returned to my task.

Sweat lined my brow, my muscles tense. Only five stitches to go. The door creaked, and I froze. Laughter erupted from the tower entrance.

*Blast*. Abandoning my tools, I slid down and lay beside the dragon.

They seemed to be having a playful argument. Eveline's voice had a flirtatious, wheedling tone. My stomach clenched. I'd never intended to be around to hear her use it on someone else.

"All right, if you insist." Eveline sounded resigned now, though still with an air of nervous excitement.

I pushed up enough to peer over Aodhan. The knight grasped Eveline's hips and lifted her atop his horse, as though she were a doll. I clenched my jaw. The man was clearly laying quite a claim to her. And why not? He'd earned the right to marry her, by her parents' standards.

He hoisted himself up behind her, possessively curling an arm around her waist. She turned to give him a shy smile. He leaned into her, placing a kiss on her forehead.

I buried my head in my hands. No point in torturing myself. When a man exuded that much charm, apparently ladies didn't bother with whether or not he fought fair.

Hoofbeats reverberated against the stone tower. My eyes flew open. The knight's steed cantered off toward the west. I exhaled. At least they wouldn't pass me or Mushroom on that path. But why west, when the royal palace was to the north?

<><><>

*(Eveline)*

The ache in my thighs dulled to numbness. I longed to stretch, to change position, to get down from this wretched horse and walk for a time. But with Batair holding me tight against his chest, the slightest shift might reveal my discomfort. The man had slain a dragon for me, the least I could do was endure a journey on horseback.

I turned my attention to the passing landscape. My view had been so limited for the past eight years that every tree and plant fascinated me, even covered in snow rather than leaves. Cold air lashed my face, and I buried my hands deeper into my fur muff. I tilted my head back to scan the sky. Knowing nothing of sorcery, I couldn't guess how Kirra might stage her attack now that the dragon no longer stood in her way. I would've felt safer if Batair had kept his armor on, but it dangled in a pack just ahead of my leg. Perhaps his eagerness to depart stemmed from a hope that we'd be long gone before she became aware of Aodhan's demise.

Batair tugged at the reins, and his horse, Perseus, slowed to a halt.

"Are we stopping for the night?" The sun angled low, a few orange rays glittering on the snow.

"Not yet, but I thought you might appreciate a break." He vaulted to the ground.

"I would. Thank you." I attempted to arrange my frozen facial muscles into a pleasant expression.

"If we ride for a few more hours, we'll reach a cave that will provide some shelter for the night."

I swallowed my groan. "That sounds perfect."

He lifted me from the saddle, his hands lingering at my sides.

My gaze paused on his face. Handsome, brave, charming, everything I'd dreamed of. And yet…well, no doubt I'd soon appreciate his frequent touch.

I glanced away. "Would you like to eat something?"

"A bit, perhaps. I don't need much after the wonderful meal you served."

Stiffness cramped my fingers and legs. After dividing half a loaf of bread and a wedge of cheese and handing him his portion, I walked up and down the path several horse-lengths before settling at his side, where he leaned against a broad tree trunk.

"You're doing well, my lady. Living in a tower mustn't lend itself to much horseback riding."

"It really doesn't." I giggled. "I likely would've fallen off by now, if not for you."

We ate in silence for a moment. I took a swig from my water flask, then tried to adopt a winning smile. "Are you ready to tell me where we're going?" I'd assumed we would head to my parents in Callidora, but he insisted on introducing me to his family first. And for some reason, he didn't want to disclose their location.

"Where would be the fun in that?" He tweaked the tip of my nose. "Don't worry, after that we'll have plenty of time to spend in your home. I just know how eager my mother is to meet you."

## Chapter 4
*(Ryker)*

Batair's horse's tracks led out of the forest, over to a rock ledge. A light in the distance caught my eye. I dismounted, then tied Mushroom's reins around a stray pine.

Straining to listen, I crept forward. Whispers of hushed conversation sounded ahead. I stepped cautiously, trying to avoid crunching the snow beneath my boots.

"So you're skilled with both a sword and a bow and arrow. You must've had a great deal of training."

Definitely Eveline. But why couldn't I see their fire?

"Mostly a lot of practice. There's little else to do as a knight, at least during times of peace." His voice was easy, jovial. As though Eveline wasn't the first maiden who'd gushed over his skill.

My hand slipped as the ledge gave way to a cavern. Batair had some mid-sized animal speared on the end of his sword, held over the fire. Eveline sat several feet away from him, her elbows planted on her knees.

All seemed well, at least for the time being.

I made my way back to Mushroom and led him to an alcove of trees. After giving him a portion of his remaining oats and water, I tore off a thick hunk of dried venison and gnawed at it. Despite being empty, my stomach didn't welcome the food.

Eveline was about to spend the night alone with that man.

Before I'd made a conscious decision, my steps headed back to the cave. The smell of roasted meat wafted in the air. Eveline licked her fingers off, then wiped them with her handkerchief. Batair rose, swiping his hands across his trousers. He crouched to dig in a pack and removed a bedroll.

My heart twisted, and I moved closer.

"I've never slept outdoors before. I could imagine it being quite pleasant, if the weather were warmer." Eveline rummaged in her own bag, producing a thick blanket.

Batair chuckled. "That does help. But if you're well prepared, winter isn't so bad." He watched Eveline lay out her blanket on the other side of the fire. "Wouldn't you rather join me on my bedroll, my lady?" His gaze swept over her appreciatively, lingering on her curves.

My fingers curled into a fist. If that swine laid a hand on her, I'd…

"No! Thank you." She flinched. "I will be quite comfortable here."

He cleared his throat. "Of course, if that is your wish."

I released a breath, easing back until I sat on my heels once more. At least the brute wasn't going to force himself on her.

They completed their nighttime preparations, the fire subsiding to a dim glow. Batair rounded to Eveline's side.

"Sleep well, Princess." He circled his arms around her and kissed her forehead. She shifted back, but he drew her closer, moving to her lips.

I dug my fingers into the snow and looked away. What was I doing here, spying on Eveline?

"Please, stop."

I glanced up. Eveline pulled away, distress in her expression.

"What's the matter, my love?"

"This is just a little too much."

"Oh." He moved his hands to her shoulders. "But we're betrothed, are we not?"

"Yes, the man who rescues me from the tower is to become my husband." She touched his face with her fingertips. "But even so, we just don't know each other that well. Yet."

"Your modesty does you credit, my lady." He released her. "Then I look forward to getting to know you better soon."

I clenched down a grunt. The gall of the man. I could only imagine how poor Eveline's cheeks must be burning.

But a satisfied grin crept in as I made my way back to Mushroom to camp for the night.

She hadn't pushed *me* away when I kissed her.

<><><>

*(Eveline)*

Morning light spilled through the cave opening. I yawned and pulled my blanket closer. I'd stayed relatively comfortable during the night, but the surrounding air was chilly.

Batair crouched over the remnants of our fire. He rubbed his hands together, then dug in his pack and removed several biscuits. After taking a bite, he glanced to me.

"Princess, you're awake."

"Yes. Good morning." I crawled out of my cocoon.

"These are a bit stale, but it's better than no breakfast at all."

I approached and accepted the two biscuits he offered. "I don't mind. Thank you."

Aside from the crackling fire and crunching of hard bread, we sat in silence.

The urge to get us past the awkwardness of the prior evening pricked me. The kiss hadn't been entirely unpleasant, but to kiss a total stranger… I tucked my arms closer to my sides. "Tell me about your mother."

"Well, she's an adoptive mother. I come from humble roots, Princess." Batair shifted. "Father was a shopkeeper's assistant, and my mother did laundry for noblewomen. Does that bother you?"

"Not at all. I'm impressed you elevated yourself to knighthood."

He nodded. "That was my adoptive mother's doing. My parents died when disease struck our town. A—benefactress, you might call her—took me in and sponsored my desire to train as a knight."

"I'm so sorry about your parents, but how generous of your adoptive mother. I'm looking forward to meeting her."

Batair removed a pot of melted snow from a stick he'd suspended above the fire. "What can you tell me about your parents?"

"If you've been training at the castle, you probably know more about them than I do." I leaned my hands toward the crackling flames, attempting to rub warmth into my fingers. "But I am impatient to see them again."

"And they, you, I'm sure." He rose, patting his legs. "Which means we'd best be off. The sooner we visit Mother, the sooner the king and queen will get their princess back."

I stood and brushed crumbs off my cloak. After we'd packed up our little camp, Batair doused the fire with the newly melted snow.

"Should be another fine travel day." He adjusted Perseus' blanket, then lifted me up to straddle the animal's neck.

My leg muscles quivered in protest. I bit my lip and squared my shoulders. The poor horse had to carry two people, plus our things. All I had to do was sit on his back.

Batair settled his hands around my waist. "Only two more days, Princess."

<><><>

*(Ryker)*

Voices carried through the still air. I'd been trailing Eveline and Batair at a distance all morning, but they must've paused for a break. I dismounted in a rush and led Mushroom in the opposite direction.

I tied Mushroom's reins around a branch in a secluded grove of trees. Thrashing in the bushes ahead had me ducking behind a wide pine.

Batair lumbered into view. I turned away, rolling my eyes. Of all the places the man could've chosen to relieve himself.

He let out a sharp whistle, and my heart took off like a spooked horse. Had he spotted me? But Batair searched the air, until an ebony raven swooped down. He extended his arm, and it landed just below his elbow.

I turned fully toward him. What in the kingdom?

"There you are at last, Fulton." I strained to hear his whisper as he stroked the bird's head. "I've been waiting to hear from Mother."

He untied a roll of paper from the bird's foot and unfurled it. After squinting at it a moment, he ripped the bottom edge in several places. Some kind of code? If only I could move closer. The raven stood still as he fastened the re-rolled paper back onto its leg.

"Take this back to her. I'll see you at the keep the day after tomorrow." He raised his arm, and with one squawk, the bird rose into the air.

The keep?

I watched the raven soar, a charcoal smudge against the icy blue sky. When it was little more than a dot on the horizon, it swerved toward the Forsaken Mountain.

*Kirra.*

My heart thundered in my ears. Batair had disappeared back through the trees.

I ran toward Mushroom, not bothering to muffle my footsteps. My fingers fumbled with the reins in my haste to untie him. He snuffled at me as I threw my leg over his back.

"Back to the tower, boy. As fast as you can go."

## Chapter 5
*(Eveline)*

The landscape became bleaker as we rode on. Even the snowflakes seemed less exuberant, as though too cold and lonely to sparkle. Still we progressed forward, up a steep mountain path.

"Your mother lives here? It looks completely uninhabited."

Batair's body rocked with his horse's movements. "She prefers a quiet life."

And quiet she got. No wonder she wanted to adopt a son.

Hours later, a structure came into view. More closely resembling a fortress than a dwelling.

"Here we are." Batair squeezed around my waist. "Home at

last."

"*This* is your home?" A strand of dread wove through my mind. "But it doesn't even look like..."

He pulled me off Perseus, gripping my arm as someone emerged from the front of the building. She beamed at us, her long, black and silver-streaked hair flowing over her shoulders. Her piercing eyes, deep blue almost to the point of purple, stirred a memory.

*Kirra.*

"No!" I pushed against him, but he tightened his hold.

"Calm down, dear girl." Kirra's voice was smooth as a velvet leaf as she approached. She raised a hand, and my body froze in place.

I struggled against the spell, but only my eyes and mouth were capable of movement.

"I have no intention of hurting you, Princess Eveline. This is a moment every woman dreams of—meeting her future daughter-in-law."

"If you think I'll marry him now..."

Kirra halted before me. "Were you not to marry the man who rescued you from the tower?"

"He was supposed to rescue me from *you*!" My head reeled. What a fool I'd been, trusting this stranger who wouldn't even tell me where we were going.

"I understand, dear. No doubt your parents told you horrid things about me, but it was all a misunderstanding. I only ever wanted to teach you."

"But—" My taut muscles eased. Presumably she could've killed me on the spot if she truly wanted me dead.

"That's better. Let's try to talk as friends."

The strange numbness covering my limbs slowly lifted. Batair eased his grasp until it no longer caused pain. Was it possible they harbored no ill will toward me?

"Let's go inside and get you two warmed up. It must've been a tedious journey." Kirra led the way into the dark, three-story structure before us.

I shuffled forward beside Batair, right into the enemy's lair.

*Father, what have I done?*

<><><>

"Would you like sugar, Princess?"

It had to be a dream. I couldn't be sitting at the dining table of Kirra's fortress while she poured my tea. "Umm, no. Thank you." The fewer opportunities I gave her to poison my drink, the better.

"Not a sweet tooth, then." She placed a steaming mug before me. "Are you hungry?"

I shook my head, but my fingers curled around my cup, drawing in warmth.

"Do you have any scones?" Batair downed his tea in two gulps. He'd been avoiding my gaze ever since we'd arrived, bearing no resemblance to the formerly confident suitor.

"Of course, knowing you were on your way." Kirra set a plate before him.

I blinked as she refilled his tea. Kirra, a *mother*. Could this be the woman my parents so feared?

With her own cup in hand, she took a seat between us. "I'm sorry, dear Eveline. I know this wasn't what you'd envisioned for your triumphant exit from that tower. You shall see your parents soon, I promise."

My tea sloshed as I raised my head. "You'll take me to them?"

"Of course. And I know Batair is anxiously anticipating the wedding."

The gentleman in question coughed and selected another scone.

I shifted against my chair. "Well, I'm not sure—"

"We won't rush you into anything. A couple should have time for courtship, after all. Once you're ready and we've made some progress with your lessons, we can make it a grand event at the palace, if you like."

"Lessons?" My mind perked up from its haze. "What kind of lessons?"

She swept out of her chair and cleared the dishes. "The art of sorcery, of course."

"No, thank you." I clasped my trembling fingers in my lap.

Kirra turned back to face me. "Being raised in Callidora has no doubt given you a negative impression of my trade. But I think you'll find you enjoy it, once you give it a chance."

"I don't intend to give it a chance. My parents—"

"Locked you in a tower for the past eight years." Kirra

resumed her seat at my side. "I apologize. This will be difficult to hear, Princess, but I fear your parents have never had your best interests in mind."

She raised a hand to stop my protest. "Of course you want to believe the best of them, but why do you think they really locked you up? Because of the threat posed by one, lonely sorceress? Or because they feared you'd make a choice they didn't agree with?" She shook her head. "It's obvious they place more value on their prejudice against magic than on their own daughter."

Something in my chest shattered. Was she right? The excuses I'd tried to make for my parents over the years had so often fallen flat. Had they been protecting me, or themselves?

Kirra gave my shoulder a tentative squeeze. "There, there, dear. I didn't mean to burden you with this on your very first day. You may have some time to think it over."

<><><>

*(Ryker)*

Mushroom grew restless as we approached Eveline's tower. I tightened my grip, urging him forward until we broke into the clearing.

Aodhan raised his head, but his eyes lacked their usual ferocity. We backed up a few steps before I dismounted and tied Mushroom to a tree. The poor horse was likely weary of such accommodations, but it was the best I could do. Fumbling to bring my pipe to my mouth, I strode back out from the tree cover. I wanted to keep the dragon awake this time, but calm enough that I wouldn't get roasted. The resulting tune was gentle and soothing, but with sufficient interest to keep the beast's eyes open.

The dragon followed my every movement. When I reached his side, I tentatively stroked a few scales. "Do you recognize me, old boy? I'm the one who stitched you up. You're still alive, so I'm hoping that means you're healing all right."

The dragon laid its head on the ground near my feet. A good sign?

"You know she's gone, don't you? I suppose you hardly know what to do with yourself now. I understand the feeling." My sigh vanished in a ghostly fog. "But Eveline needs our help, Aodhan."

He'd raised his head at the sound of Eveline's name.

Hope swelled in my chest. "Will you come with me?"

He blew out a wisp of fire.

I jerked but steadied myself. Maybe it was time for more music. I played a livelier tune, entreating the dragon to rise and find a new purpose. He stood, gingerly shaking out his wings. My heart sank. After Batair's butchery, would he even be able to fly? I made my way to one side, still playing. The thick gauziness of his wing was bunched where I'd removed the dagger, but no hole remained.

I returned to the dragon's head, careful to stay to the side of his massive jaws. Increasing the pace of my song, I encouraged him to walk away from the tower, to the edge of the tree cover. "Now stay here for a moment, I'll be right back."

With the front entrance clear, I ran to Mushroom and got him situated with food, water, and a blanket in the tower stall. "I'll come back for you as soon as I can." He nuzzled my hand before shifting his attention to the bag of oats. I gave him one last pat, then jogged out into the waning sunshine.

Aodhan stomped in place, smoke emanating from his mouth. I played a gentle tune as I approached. "Just me again." I patted his scales, trying not to wince as the jagged edges caught my hand. "I know you were hurt recently, but do you think you can fly?"

He puffed his chest and gave his wings a quick flap.

"Excellent. But I also need to ride on your back."

The dragon curved his neck to look me in the eye. The intelligence there was always startling. It blinked slowly, then crouched. I awkwardly ascended, grasping at scales to propel myself upward. Aodhan swatted my backside with his wing, heaving me fully onto his back. I settled in, clinging to his neck but careful to stay above the puckered black gash. "He's taking her to the Forsaken Mountain."

Aodhan shuddered beneath me, then the muscles in his shoulders tensed, his wings rousing the snow in flurries around us. I laid my head against his neck and squeezed my eyes closed.

*Eveline, I'm going to do everything I can to keep you from Kirra.* The dragon's speed increased as cold air tried to pry me from his back. *Or die trying.*

**Chapter 6**
*(Eveline)*

A shaft of moonlight angling through the window above my bed illuminated my blankets. My second night in the keep. Kirra had continued to see to my every comfort, and Batair's courtship had turned sweet and shy. I would've been thrilled with my situation, if my knight hadn't taken me to my parents' greatest enemy. If Kirra hadn't announced magic lessons would start tomorrow.

Sitting up, I raised my pillow to cushion my headboard. Would I participate in the lessons? Admittedly, I couldn't help being curious about what kind of power her instruction might unleash. Did sorcery have to be bad? My parents hadn't kept me home long enough to explain why they objected so strongly. Why their opposition was worth locking me in a tower for almost half my life.

I folded my arms across my chest, but Ryker's soft voice drifted through my gloom. *Your parents love you. I believe they tried to do what was right.* Though I'd often felt like a sacrifice, would I have felt the same way if they'd given me up to Kirra as a pupil instead? They'd at least stood by their consciences in their decision.

Dear Ryker. A hint of a smile flitted over my lips. Less than a week ago we'd laughed together, speculated about whether my knight would ever come.

How quickly it had all gone wrong.

Closing my eyes, I leaned my head back. *Spirit, guide me with Your wisdom.* My tutor had insisted magic went against the Holy Trinity. Through it, humans grasp at the Father's power but instead only slip further into darkness.

I blew out a sigh. *Then I should decline?* A knot formed in my stomach, but a thread of peace gently loosened it. Perhaps Kirra wouldn't take it badly. And even if she did, my parents had been brave enough to defy her.

I would be, too.

<><><>

"Breakfast is ready."

My fingers trembled as I fastened the last button of my dress. "I'll be down in a moment."

Kirra greeted me at the bottom of the stairs, her brows raised. "Our meal will be brief. We have a full day ahead of us."

I grasped my skirt to hide my shaking hands. "Actually, I

wanted to speak with you about that. I gave it some thought last night, and while I truly appreciate your offer to take me on as your student, I would prefer not to learn sorcery."

She opened and closed her mouth before speaking. "But Eveline, dear, it couldn't hurt to at least give it a try."

"It could, and I'd rather not. I understand if my decision means I'm no longer welcome to your hospitality."

Batair paused on his way to the kitchen, his wide eyes fixed on his mother.

Kirra swallowed. "*Decision* is a very strong word. You may have a bit more time to consider, if you must, but we really should—"

"Thank you, but I don't need more time. I will not go against the Holy Trinity in this, and nothing will change my mind." I squared my shoulders.

"I see." Kirra pressed her lips together. "I'm sorry to hear that, as it requires me to revert to my alternative course of action. A course that could prove much more detrimental to your family."

My heart stuttered. "What course of action is that?"

"You will return to the Callidorian palace as a sorceress, in one way or another."

"You're going to bring me with you?"

She snorted. "No, Princess. I will go as you."

My mind grasped for an explanation. "But…how?"

"Just think what I could've taught you." Kirra stepped forward, but only to tweak my chin. "Then this is what you want? For me to go in your place and unleash my wrath upon your family?" She shook her head. "The poor things will think their daughter lost her mind locked up in that tower for so long."

Horror washed over me. "No, please."

She tilted her head. "Then we may proceed with our lessons?"

*Father, Son, Spirit, what can I do?* Either way, I'd betray my parents. But would succumbing to Kirra's plans at least keep them safe?

*You know the right path*. The whisper took root in my heart, blossoming outward like a whorl bush.

I curled my fingers into fists. "I do not wish to learn any magic."

"Very well." She grasped my arm, rifling in her pocket with

her free hand. Removing a razor, she sliced into the tip of my finger.

I cried out, struggling against her.

"Batair, come hold her."

A muscle in his jaw tightened, then he crossed the room to us. He gripped my shoulders, holding me immobile as she held a vial to my bleeding finger.

I angled my head toward him. "Batair, please. Help me." The slightest sound escaped on my breath.

A sad expression crossed his face before it hardened. "I'm afraid, Princess, we really don't know each other that well."

Tears stung my eyes. Throwing my own words back at me. He wasn't worth my regret, that was certain. I raised my voice. "Release me this instant. When my father finds out harm has come to me, he will—"

"Your father has no control over me, child." Kirra narrowed her eyes as one last crimson drop flowed into the vial. "But there's no cause for dramatics, that's all I needed." She swiped a handkerchief over my injury, then popped a small cork into the container's opening. "Now, Batair, take her to her room and make sure she stays there. I have work to do."

<><><>

Locked in again, with less freedom than ever. The urge to throw my lamp against the wall nearly overtook me, but I didn't dare draw more attention to myself than necessary. So, I settled for pacing across the rug. Batair and Kirra had thus far delivered four meals to my door. How many more would I eat as a prisoner?

I dropped onto the bed, leaned my face into the pillow, and screamed. A guttural cry followed from elsewhere in the keep, making me jump. Why would anyone else be shouting? Another loud grunt, followed by footsteps. Kirra must've been in her workshop, which shared a wall with my cell. Batair's voice mingled with hers, questioning, then soothing.

Steps pounded through the hall again, halting outside my door. My throat constricted as I replaced my pillow and rose. How did I manage to anger her this time?

The bolt scraped and clicked, and Kirra stormed in with Batair on her heels.

"What have you done?" Kirra pointed at me.

"N-nothing." I leaned away from her sharp fingernail. "What

could I do, trapped in this chamber like a criminal?"

"The potion was brewing just fine. I completed every step with precision." She clenched her hands into fists. "Then, with no provocation, it stopped. You must've—"

Her words trailed off as she rushed to the window behind me.

## Chapter 7
*(Ryker)*

If I'd ever wished to experience flight, the desire fled the moment Aodhan took to the air. My stomach remained a horse-length behind the rest of my body, and the wind threatened to whip me off his back every time the dragon beat his wings. Aodhan apparently understood my combination of yells and arm waves well enough to determine which direction we needed to travel. The Forsaken Mountain loomed ahead.

I clung to Aodhan's back as we began a gradual descent. A sturdy gray building came into view below. Well-constructed, but cold and ominous.

His scales scraped my hand as I clutched tighter. "Down there!" My shout trailed off in a gust of wind, but Aodhan's bulky head lunged downward.

His feet crashed into the ground with a thud, making his entire body vibrate. After several swallows, I peeked out. We'd landed in a clearing right next to the dark structure. A new surge of panic coursed through my veins. Now what? Beyond the dragon, I hadn't devised a plan. Should we have landed elsewhere? Or waited until the cover of darkness?

A door creaked open, followed by a jumble of loud voices. *Too late now.*

"Ryker!" Eveline rounded the corner of the fortress, arms outstretched. My heart rate paused in its incessant staccato. She was alive, unharmed. I slid down Aodhan's back. That embrace would be worth every—

Batair trudged into view, followed by a tall woman in a dress of deep crimson. The knight grasped Eveline's arm and tugged her back. Her responding glare would've melted icicles off the roof.

I let my breath expand my chest, then strode forward. "Release the princess to me. Now." Even with a dragon at my side, I couldn't manage to sound threatening.

The woman, presumably Kirra, raised an eyebrow. "Who is this boy?"

"The one who puts the dragon to sleep." Batair eyed Aodhan with a mixture of confusion and alarm.

"The dragon you failed to kill, I see." Kirra narrowed her eyes at him.

"This can remain peaceful, if you allow the princess to come to me."

Eveline strained forward, but Batair clamped a fist around her other wrist. Bile soured my throat.

"I'm afraid we have need of her." Kirra's voice rivaled the frosty air.

The mere presence of a dragon apparently wasn't enough. I drew Aodhan's head lower. "Don't hurt anyone, but could you scare them? Just a little?"

He jerked his head back, then roared with an eruption of flame.

I blinked at the sudden brightness against the gloomy sky. "You'd best not anger him further—he can be unpredictable." I crossed my arms to hide my shaking hands. "Let the princess go, and he won't hurt anyone." *Probably*.

Kirra moved next to Eveline. "Your bravado is all very amusing, but I'm growing weary of your antics."

"Then just release—"

"No, it's my turn to make demands." Something silver flashed in her hand as she raised it to Eveline's neck. "Remove the dragon, or I slit the princess's throat."

Eveline tugged harder against Batair, but he held firm. "You won't be getting any more of my blood." She kicked backward, and Batair hissed a curse.

"Enough." Kirra slashed the knife.

Eveline whimpered as a line of red darkened her ivory neck.

"No, don't hurt her. Please." I stared at the wound. Even with a dragon as an ally, while Eveline was at their mercy, I was helpless.

"We have no desire to hurt her." Kirra stroked a thumb along the hilt of her dagger. "Take this dragon far from the Forsaken Mountain, and she will remain unharmed. Batair will stay here with the princess during my journey to the Callidorian palace. He will know how to act, should you be foolish enough to bring that fiend anywhere near this keep ever again."

Resignation saddened Eveline's eyes, but not fear. Brave, wonderful girl.

I tried to convey all my love and apology in one long look before turning to Kirra. "You have my word."

"Good." Kirra's satisfied smile brought to mind a shadow fox returned from a successful hunt. "Batair, Princess, let us retire to our chambers. I trust I may resume my potion-making shortly." She tucked the dagger into the folds of her dress before marching toward the door.

Eveline twisted her head to regard me once more as Batair shoved her from behind.

Tears forged icy trails down my cheeks the moment they disappeared from sight. I'd failed her. I'd flown in on a dragon, yet was still too much of a cowardly imbecile to rescue her.

Aodhan stomped at my side.

My head drooped. "I'm so sorry, boy."

He nudged my shoulder with his chin.

"Thanks. But we need to get you out of here." *You*. My mind grasped at the word.

Perhaps hope wasn't lost, after all.

<><><>

*(Eveline)*

I tugged again, tearing off a thin strip. Kirra had departed hours before for the palace, leaving Batair to guard me in the keep. My heart ached, picturing the despair on Ryker's face. We'd been so close. But with Ryker as my inspiration, I was determined to rescue myself. If I could turn these torn up sheets into a rope and escape out the window…

My posture slumped, and I set my work in my lap. Then what? I'd wander aimlessly through the wintry forest until I perished?

I shook my head. Even if it wasn't a foolproof plan, I had to try. Taking up my ruined sheets once more, I gave a vigorous yank.

Something pounded on the door at the foot of the stairs. Had Kirra returned so soon? Perhaps my parents sent someone looking for me. I peered out my window, but all was dark. This vantage point didn't reveal the outer door, anyway. My hands trembled with combined trepidation and excitement as I resumed my work, straining to listen.

Batair stomped down the stairway, grumbling. A minute later, the heavy wooden door groaned open, and he called something into the void. I tiptoed to my chamber door and pressed my ear to the coarse wood.

Muffled sounds continued to disturb the quiet evening. Batair let out a distant cry, and the front door slammed shut. Wood clattered as someone secured the thick beam across the entryway.

I leaned against the door, my breaths panting in quick succession. My captor's absence filled me with a thrill, but dread nagged at the corners of my mind. Would the newcomer prove to be my salvation? Or an even worse threat?

A voice rang up from the entrance. "Eveline? Are you there?"

*Ryker*. "Up here!" I pounded on the hard wood.

He tinkered with the lock until the door burst open. Trembling, he wrapped his arms around me. "Thank the Father you're alive." He peered into my face. "Did they harm you?"

"No." I nestled against his chest. "Kirra's gone. The potion worked, so she set off toward the palace. Looking just like—" Suppressed tears choked off my words.

Ry stroked his fingers through my hair. "We'll find a way to stop her."

"But you promised you wouldn't come back. And how did you get Batair out?" I stepped away from him.

"Actually, I promised to keep Aodhan away." He waggled his eyebrows. "They never said I couldn't return on foot."

Laughter felt so freeing. I looped my arm under his elbow and squeezed his fingers.

He started slightly, then encased my hand with both of his. "As for Batair, did I ever tell you I can throw my voice?"

"What do you mean?"

He opened his mouth, and a cry reminiscent of a lark sounded down the hall.

I jerked. "That was you? But how—?"

"Just another of my musical gifts." He grinned. "Anyway, I lured him outside, then ran in and bolted the door behind me."

"Impressive."

He caught my gaze, and pink tinted his ears. "Well, it was a start. Aodhan's waiting for us a few hours' walk away. But we need to get out, and I doubt the front entrance is an option."

"I have an idea." I hurried to the bed and retrieved my homemade rope. "Do you think this might work?"

A slow smile spread across his face. "Brilliant." He grasped my shoulders and pressed a kiss to my forehead. Then he stepped back, the blush spreading to redden his face. "Sorry, I shouldn't take such liberties."

Warmth forced its way into my own cheeks. "I don't mind."

"Truly?" His smile was achingly hopeful. "Eveline, I..."

A series of thumps shook the front door.

I let out a breathy giggle. "We should really get back to—"

"Right." He coughed and took the rope from my hands. "Seems strong enough to hold us if we go one at a time." He paused at the edge of the bed. "Do you mind?"

"Not at all."

He swallowed and climbed up onto the mattress. When he reached the wall, he rose to his knees to study the window. "Does this open without force?"

"Yes, but I haven't tested how far." I hovered near my pillow, rising to my tiptoes to watch his movements.

"Then let's try it." He wrenched at the window, and it gave way. First a crack, then just enough for him to squeeze his shoulders through. "Barely, but it'll suffice."

I passed him one end of the tied-together bedsheets. He lowered it out the window, while I stood on the bed to loop the other end around a ceiling beam.

Ry smiled up at me. "I'll catch you at the bottom."

I didn't formulate a response before he grasped the rope in both hands and eased out the window. Kneeling at the ledge, I watched his descent, ready to grab the rope if my knot didn't hold.

He jumped the last few feet to the ground, then waved to me.

Tucking my skirt between my legs, I forced myself out the window. The narrow opening compressed my chest tighter than a corset. Once through, I clung to the rope and rooted my gaze to the wall. *Don't look down. Don't look down.* My hands inched along the fabric. A chill wind blew hair into my face. I spit it out and moved my hands faster.

After what felt like an eternity, a soothing voice whispered nearby, "That's it, Ev. You're almost there." Ryker clasped my waist and helped me ease the rest of the way down. "Atta girl. Let's be on our way." He took my hand, and we ran for the nearest tree cover. The moonlit trees stretched eerily before us, a web of tangled, bony branches. But nothing could be worse than the nightmare I left behind.

We broke into the forest and slowed to a brisk walk. I exhaled a shaky breath. *This might actually work.*

A large figure stepped out of the shadows into our path. "Just how dull-witted do you think I am?"

<><><>

*(Ryker)*

Batair loomed before us, a scowl replacing his usual smirk. He drew his sword from its sheath with an ominous ring. "It's time to put an end to these pathetic rescue efforts."

He swung the blade at me, and I dove behind a tree. I dug through the snow in a desperate attempt to find something useful. Rising, I held out a wide stick between both hands just as he struck again. The sword sliced through my feeble excuse for a weapon, but I bashed half the severed branch into his face. He faltered, and I climbed onto his back, my arms clamped around his neck.

Eveline stood frozen, her eyes lit with panic.

"Run, Eveline!" My yell tore through the surrounding silence. "You're the one they want."

"But I can't..."

"Just go!"

With a determined nod, she whirled and took off in the direction of the keep.

Batair roared, brandishing his sword as I tightened my grip around his neck. The blade sliced through my coat sleeve as though it were made of netting. Pain scorched my veins, but I choked back a cry. Shifting my uninjured arm further around Batair's throat, I loosened my grip with the other and clawed at his face.

With a series of grunts and curses, he ducked to the ground and rolled until he crushed me into a layer of snow. He twisted and leaned heavily on my neck. I flailed, but his weight pressed upon my lungs, turning my breaths to gasps. My struggle slowed, until my lungs convulsed and black spots danced across my vision.

Just as my consciousness began to slip away, the pressure lifted. I pried my eyes open. Batair stood over me, his sword tip hovering above my chest.

"Was it worth it, flute boy? Risking your life to save a woman who'd run out on you the moment she got a chance?"

"At least she likes me better than you." Wheezes punctuated my words.

His brows lowered at a steep angle. "What do you suppose she was thinking as she ran, after seeing you clinging to me like a leech instead of fighting like a man?" He kicked my leg. "It's amusing you thought any of your pathetic plans might work."

I closed my eyes, trying to block out his words. I'd always known I wasn't the rescuing type. So why had I bothered to try, when failure was inevitable? I should've flown Aodhan off to get a true knight to come back and save her. Icy moisture seeped through my clothes, chilling my skin.

My foolish charade would be over soon enough.

"Your dainty princess won't last a day in the wilderness on her own." His sneer churned my insides. "Maybe I'll make her return to the tower a bit more interesting."

*No*! Eveline needed more time to escape. I began to shift out from under the blade, keeping my expression pained.

"She is a pretty little thing, and…" He staggered as something slammed into him from behind. A second blow sent him lurching to his knees.

I grasped the flat sides of his sword and jerked it from his hands. Scrambling to stand, I fumbled with the weapon until my shaky fists clutched the hilt.

Batair growled as his wrists were yanked behind him. A large, heavy board sank into the snow at his side.

"You'd best allow me to tie up your hands, Sir Batair, unless you'd like Ryker to persuade you." Never before had Eveline's voice sounded so angelic.

I stuck the blade against the knight's broad neck. "You came back."

"Of course I came back." She shot me a glare over his shoulder. "You didn't think I'd abandon you to this brute, did you?"

"I wouldn't have blamed you."

Cloth draped over Batair's eyes. A cute set of grunts accompanied her efforts to tie the blindfold at the back of his head. "I would've blamed myself plenty." She wrapped another piece of cloth around his mouth, muffling his string of curses. "That's enough out of you."

I pressed more of the blade against his throat.

He mumbled something against the gag. His posture remained taut, but he stilled.

I shifted the heavy sword to my other hand. "What next? Are we going to leave him here?"

She gnawed at her lip. "Tempting, but we probably shouldn't let him freeze to death." She checked the knots securing his hands. "Batair, if you're willing to cooperate, we'll take you back inside the keep. If not, we'll have to abandon you here to suffer the elements. Do you understand?"

He nodded slightly, avoiding pressing his jaw against the sword.

"Good." Eveline positioned herself at his side and pulled him to his feet. "When you feel the sword at your back, you walk."

We marched him awkwardly back to the tower, through the door, and up the stairs to the room Eveline indicated as his chamber. After using more of the torn bedsheets to tie his ankles together and secure him to a chair, we closed the door behind us and maneuvered the plank from the front entrance to block the handle.

"Let's get out of here." I lowered the sword into the sheath I'd snatched from Batair's waistband.

"Yes, please." Eveline placed a quick kiss on my cheek before taking my hand and flinging open the front door.

My face tingled where her lips had touched, and my fingers warmed, encased by hers. Eveline came back for me, and I had rescued her, in my own ungainly manner. I glanced down—her gaze radiated admiration and trust. Just maybe...

A ray of hope dawned in my mind like a glorious sunrise.

## Chapter 8
*(Eveline)*

Hoofbeats clipped against the gravel up ahead. I urged my feet faster, stumbling in a few deeper patches of snow. Ryker walked with Aodhan farther from the path, waiting for my signal. I pushed aside evergreen boughs to peer through. A girl with regal bearing and long, blonde hair rippling down her back rode sidesaddle atop a large, black horse. My face, reflected back to me as though in a cursed mirror. Chin raised high, eyes haughty and cold.

Ugh, I hoped such an expression had never crossed *my* features.

Raising my pipe to my lips, I played the four-note tune Ryker had taught me.

Snow stirred as Aodhan took flight several horse-lengths away. Frantic whinnies sounded from the path.

My heart thudded so loudly it seemed to reside in my ears. Would Kirra out-maneuver us yet again, even without Batair? I ran forward.

"…warned you, foolish boy." Kirra sat tall, despite the jostling from her mount. "Your princess will die for this mistake. I'll send word to Batair at once, unless you—"

"I'm not sure your message will be received." I stepped into Kirra's line of sight.

Ryker tried to motion me back into hiding, but I stood firm. I wouldn't let Kirra frighten me anymore.

Her confident stance faltered. "What have you done to him?"

At least she was enough of a mother to have concern for her adopted son. "He should be fine. Though probably hungry and weary of being tied up. I suggest you return to him right away."

She tugged Perseus' reins, turning him fully toward me. "What a mistake, letting you live. But this isn't over, Princess. I still have plenty of potion, and I—"

"Ryker, no!"

Aodhan's face hovered just above Kirra, his jaws wide. No matter her faults, I couldn't watch the sorceress be eaten alive.

She screamed and covered her head with her hands.

Ryker's steady gaze met mine. "Trust me." He patted the dragon's neck, whispering in his ear. Aodhan's mouth closed most of the way, keeping only Kirra's raised hand between his teeth. Under Ryker's guidance, he eased his jaw closed, piercing the skin of her finger but leaving it otherwise intact. With a smoke-filled snort, Aodhan released her, shook his head, and stepped back.

Kirra had moaned when her finger was bitten, but now raised her head. I clasped a hand over my mouth. Her green eyes had returned to indigo, and brown darkened her hair and brows. She studied the marks on her hand, then caught up the ends of her hair with a screech. "The potion! What did that beast do to me?"

Ryker pressed his lips together. "Turns out my theory was right. The bite of a dragon removed your magic. My hope is that it will also render any further sorcery attempts fruitless. Only time will tell." He shrugged, and his chest puffed out a bit. "I'd be happy to repeat the process in the future if necessary, as I plan to keep Aodhan near the princess at all times."

Kirra, now looking entirely like herself, glowered at him. "Dragon or not, you will not be rid of me so easily."

"Believe me, it wasn't easy." Ryker chuckled. "You'd best go see to your son, and if you insist on taking on a pupil, find one elsewhere."

Kirra's shoulders sagged. "You didn't hurt him?"

I glanced up to meet her eyes as I crossed to Ryker. "Batair is unharmed."

She nodded, keeping her head down.

"Ready to go home, Ev?" Ryker nudged my side.

Instead of taking his offered hand, I twined my arms around his neck.

<><><>

The doors to the throne room appeared much less imposing than when I'd last seen them eight years before. Ryker had directed Aodhan to a cave a good distance from the palace, then lured him into a much-deserved sleep with his pipe. We'd taken the remainder of the journey on foot. I wiggled my sore, swollen toes in my boots. Hopefully, my welcome back to the palace would include a long, hot bath.

The guards, like everyone else we'd passed, regarded me with a mixture of confusion and awe. One paused as he reached for the engraved handle of the large wooden door. "Are you sure you wouldn't like me to announce you first, Your Majesty?"

My parents were apparently in the midst of a private dinner. "No, thank you."

He nodded and heaved the door open. I tightened my grip on Ryker's hand.

Father dropped his fork and stood, frowning. "What is the meaning of this? Interrupting a..."

His voice trailed off as we stared at each other across the room. He'd grown a beard, and his doublet fit more snugly than before. Mother stood on the other side of their bewildered guests. The same gentle manner, but her hair had acquired a few streaks of white, her face a few more wrinkles.

Forcing back regret over the years lost, I ran forward.

Mother caught me first, her tight squeeze deflating my lungs like a bagpipe. "Eveline, darling, it is you! Home at last."

"I can't tell you how we've longed for this moment." Father embraced us both, his voice hoarse. "I apologize we didn't receive you properly, I'd expected some kind of notice…"

I hugged them tighter, letting their affection wash over me like a healing balm over my wounds from the separation.

Mother swiped her tapered sleeve under her eyes. "I've wondered so many times if we were right to send you away." She kissed my cheek. "Well, best to put that all behind us now. We can't wait to meet your—"

Father's eyes narrowed as he gazed behind me. "Ryker. You ought to have returned over a week ago. What is the meaning of this?"

I clutched Father's arm. "Ryker brought me back because he saved me."

He shook his head. "That's not how this arrangement was to work, and the boy knows it."

"But he's the one I want to marry."

Father's "What?" nearly drowned out Ryker's squeak.

Ryker took a few tentative steps forward. "I—I am?"

"Yes." I reached for him, then stopped. "That is, I hoped you'd want to marry me."

"I do." His vigorous nod shook a lock of hair over his forehead. He took my hands, his voice lowering to a whisper. "I've dreamed of little else for years."

A miniature dragon soared through my chest, leaving me elated and dizzy.

"No, no, no." Father glowered at Ryker. "You were to put the beast to sleep for your deliveries only, not to slay him yourself and apparently woo my daughter. You have betrayed our trust to—"

"He hasn't, Father." I put some distance between myself and Ryker. "He saved me—not from the dragon, but directly from

Kirra's keep."

Father rubbed his forehead. "From Kirra? But..."

"I promise to explain everything soon." I patted his arm before placing myself at Ryker's side. "All you need to know for now is that Ryker was braver than any man I've ever seen. He risked everything for me. And he did it all with kindness and compassion, never raising a sword against an innocent creature."

Ryker's intense gaze made my stomach clench.

"But—but he's not a knight."

I'd forgotten how stubborn Father could be. "Isn't following the Son's example of bravery even more noble than battling with weapons and armor?"

"It certainly is." Mother laid a hand on Father's back.

Father slumped his shoulders. "We're just trying to keep you safe."

"If I may, Your Highness," Ryker cleared his throat, "Aodhan is now trained to obey my commands. Most of them, anyway. If we're allowed to stay, he ought to be able to prevent Kirra, or any other sorceress, from exerting power near the palace."

"Trained, you say?" Father scratched his beard. "Do you think you could train other dragons?"

"I'd certainly be willing to try."

"Just think...if we could use dragons instead of fight them. It'd be revolutionary." He straightened his collar. "We must discuss this further."

Ryker nodded, eyes wide. "Of course, Your Majesty."

Mother extended a hand to him. "It sounds as though you've proven yourself a worthy husband for our daughter, young man. Welcome to the family."

His voice shook as he lightly kissed the backs of her fingers. "Thank you, Your Highness."

<><><>

I leaned into Ryker, inhaling his woodsy scent. Following a joyous reunion with other members of my family and days of celebration, we finally had an opportunity to relax. Alone.

He circled his arm around my shoulders, gliding his hand through my hair. "I still can hardly believe it. You don't know how often I've longed for a moment like this."

"Truly?" I straightened. "I had no idea you harbored such feelings. At least, not until you kissed me."

He chuckled and pressed his lips to my forehead. "I know. I pined away for years, while you remained blissfully unaware."

My heart dipped. "I'm so sorry, Ry. I should've paid more attention."

"No, it was just as well. I had no grounds to declare my feelings for you or hope for any reciprocation."

"Ugh, I've been so blind." I buried my head in his shoulder. "I don't know how I couldn't see it before. It's just…my parents' plan, the one I grew up relying on. It made sense, in its way."

My gaze landed on the tapestry of the Son at birth and death. One of the many items from the tower that had been transferred to my new palace living quarters by Ryker's faithful Mushroom. "You'd think I would've learned by now that the Father's plans tend to look nothing like my own."

"You're not the only one. Don't forget, I didn't exactly intend to rescue you." He shifted away to face me. "But Ev, if this isn't the outcome you hoped for… If the bravest, strongest knight is still who you want, you could always have that tournament you talked about."

"Hold your tongue." I frowned, raising a finger over his mouth. "Don't even mention such a thing. I had the strongest knight, and he made me feel anything but safe." I placed a hand on either side of Ryker's face. "It's true you're nothing like the man I thought I wanted to marry. But I wouldn't change a thing."

"I can't tell you how happy I am to hear that."

I melted into him the moment our lips met. At length he released me, the ardor in his eyes turning my insides to mush.

"Besides," I brushed the hair from his forehead, "what man would dare challenge the bravery of my dragon-trainer fiancé?"

"Only a very foolish one." A grin lit his face before he leaned in for another kiss.

# Cookies & Cream Fudge

I felt so lost the first Christmas after we discovered our son has egg and nut allergies, since all of my go-to holiday dessert recipes included one or both. **Cookies & Cream Fudge** quickly became a new family favorite and is now requested by my kids every year! Easy and delicious.

**Ingredients:**

18 ounces white chocolate

1 (14 ounce) can sweetened condensed milk

1/8 teaspoon salt

3 cups crème-filled chocolate sandwich cookies, broken into fourths

**Directions:**

1. Line an 8-inch square pan with wax paper.
2. Combine white chocolate, sweetened condensed milk, and salt in a saucepan, and melt over low heat.
3. Stir in cookie pieces.
4. Spread evenly into pan, and chill for two hours or until firm.
5. Turn the fudge onto a cutting board, peel off the wax paper, and cut into squares. Refrigerate leftovers—if you have any!

<><><>

Find Laurie Lucking online:

***Website address: www.laurielucking.com***
***Facebook address: www.facebook.com/AuthorLaurieLucking/***
***Twitter handle @LaurieLucking***

***Blog address: www.landsuncharted.com***
***Instagram handle: @LaurieLucking***

# Crystal Christmas

### *By Michelle L. Levigne*

*Sequel to **Music in the Night**,*
*Part of the Guardians of the Time Stream series.*

*December 1878*
*Cleveland, Ohio*

Sneaking up on Brogan Ambrose was impossible. Thanks to the song growing between him and Carmen Mackenzie, they always knew where each other was in the tunnel community below the growing port city. The song of the crystal dust and slivers embedded in his face merged with the notes from the crystal rose in the cross Carmen never took off, creating new notes that expanded into the promise of a majestic chord. The growth was as gradual as seeds, smaller than dust, germinating below the snow. That sense of his presence was a comfort, and often a sweet, secret joy.

Even now, when the pleasant sensation had taken on a bit of a mysterious tint. Carmen had the growing suspicion that the bond between them, both of the heart and mind, was being aided by the as-yet-to-be fully understood properties of crystal. Anything was possible. After all, this was the same crystal that had composed the Great Machine that brought their ancestors from the far distant future to the even farther distant past. Lately, she suspected Brogan's thoughts were somehow leaking into her mind. Aided by crystal.

In a few moments, she would have her proof. A hazy picture had formed in her mind over the last ten minutes or so of the children's music class. An image of Brogan coming down this tunnel to meet with Mr. Ransom Wallace. There was no logical reason for the head investigator of the law firm of Endicott, Lewis and MacDonald to come down into the tunnel community in the middle of the day, unless he and Brogan were conspiring about something.

That something had to do with crystal. Carmen was sure of it. The hazy impressions over the last few days had grown clearer, like adjusting the extending sections of a mariner's telescope until details grew sharp enough to discern. It helped that Brogan had been thinking of her in relation to crystal, and Ransom, and Ess Fremont. Carmen couldn't be absolutely sure, but she thought the focus on Ess came from Ransom. She quite approved of the clever, brave man's growing dedication to Ess, her make-believe childhood friend who had proved real at the perfect moment in God's timing. She found it quite delightful when mentioning Ransom to Ess sometimes made her clever, confident friend lose her train of thought, or even blush.

A soft shimmer of energy from the crystal rose tucked under her shirt tugged Carmen out of her thoughts. She sat up a little straighter on the bench in the alcove here in the knotted intersection of the tunnels, where she was sure Brogan was coming to meet Ransom. A little bit of thought, and the crystal's energy let her "see" Brogan coming up from the tunnel to the right. He walked in darkness, guided by his sharp senses, intimate knowledge of the tunnels, and crystal energy. Carmen allowed herself a tiny smile of pride that she walked without candle or lantern as well now. Her lessons in using the crystal of the ancestors, expanding on the gift she had inherited from her mother, had progressed even more rapidly than she and Ess had dared dream. Seeing through crystal was just the tip of the proverbial iceberg -- at least, that was the saying she had picked up from some of the sailors among the Originators, who had come to take their winter's rest in the tunnels. This winter was proving to be unusually bitter, and Lake Erie threatened to freeze solid, even around the busy port of Cleveland.

"Waiting in ambush, are you?" Brogan's voice was a deep, rich rumble of muted laughter.

"I know better. And so do you." Carmen held her breath as she focused her will on the shards of crystal embedded in the ceiling of the intersection of seven tunnels. Light slowly grew, blue-tinged white, spilling down to touch Brogan as he emerged from the tunnel.

"Indeed I do." He chuckled and caught up her hand to hold between both of his and settled onto the bench next to her. "The question, I suppose, is which of us is doing the mental leaking."

"Oh, what a terrible image." She wrinkled her nose at him when he laughed. "Matilda says it isn't leaking, but growing together, into harmony. I much prefer that musical image."

"Indeed, so do I." He squeezed her hand. "Do you mind? Because I don't. Mind. At all," he hurried to say.

"Not a wit." With another twitch of her nose, she reached up with her free hand to stroke the waxy-looking skin on his left cheek. The impression that he had been burned was all that remained of the horrible scarring and disfigurement that had prompted him to hide in the darkness for years. It was still a sweet joke between them that nobody but Carmen noticed when her musical talent combined with crystal had begun healing those scars.

"Songbird," he whispered, and pressed his hand over hers, holding it against his cheek.

Crystal shimmered silent music through their blood. Through his ears, she heard footsteps coming down a tunnel to the left. It led up to the sheltered entrance, within the slowly growing Tower belonging to the Originators.

"Heard that, did you?" He turned his head enough to brush a kiss against her palm, then released her hand, sighed, and stood.

"Mr. Wallace is coming, and the two of you are conspiring over something. I have the impression you want to ask me ... to help you?"

"We're running out of options, and the only people left who we can ask, if you can't assist us, are the last ones we want to contact. The *Golden Nile* is due in ten days. Even if we can get help from Miss Athena, there might not be enough time to accomplish our task. Not for Ransom's deadline."

"You're putting a present together for Ess, aren't you?" Carmen guessed.

The airship that was the core of the Originators' growing fleet would be the first to dock at the Tower, which had reached the height of four stories. A scaffolding was being erected as a makeshift docking tower, in defiance of the fierce winter winds attacking Cleveland since the start of November. The entire Fremont family had been traveling on the airship for the last three months, conferring with different groups among the Originators. The Tower was intended to be their headquarters, since the destruction more than a year ago of Sanctuary, the former headquarters near San Francisco. Overcoming the centuries of secrecy and maintaining small cells to hide from the Revisionists was a slow-moving task. The Fremonts, especially Ernest and Matilda, carried most of that burden. Ess and her brother, Uly, had put aside their own projects to support their grandparents. They had earned a month or two of rest, and the coming holidays were the perfect time.

"If you can provide us the --" Brogan stiffened and turned to look down the tunnel.

Carmen swore she saw a tiny spark of light, in the deepest groove of scarring along his cheekbone. As if crystal peered out from his bone. She shivered, aching for the suffering he had endured for so long.

"What's wrong?" she whispered.

Brogan shook his head and hurried down the tunnel, vanishing from the bubble of light filling the intersection. A moment later, he was back, with Mouse, half-wrapped in a blanket, cradled in his arms. Ransom followed them. Carmen stood, fighting a shiver. The first time she had seen the adventurous little girl, Mouse had fallen and broken her leg while exploring a half-demolished building. The same building Carmen and her tribe of orphans had taken shelter in. She had done the only thing she could do, pray and sing over Mouse. Healing had flowed through her when she yielded herself fully to the Lord's service, aided by the crystal rose in her mother's cross. That chance meeting and miraculous healing had eventually led to them being right here: underground, safe and sheltered from the storm settling in over Lake Erie and Cleveland.

"One of our messengers from Miss Hilda's came to get me. They found her curled up in a doorway, shivering hard enough to knock all her bones loose," Ransom said. "Nobody'd go near her. Rumors are growing about some wretched killing fever drifting through the city. Said some sailors jumped a sick airship before the officials could quarantine it and lock it down. Carrying a plague from Europe, according to the alarmists." His mouth twisted like he might want to spit, but his hand was gentle as he brushed sweaty hair off Mouse's pale forehead. "I couldn't drop her in one of the charity wards up above, could I? Even if I'm bringing that fever down here, her chances are still better. And so are yours. Right?"

"Absolutely." Carmen wrapped her arms around herself and fought to stand up straight, when she wanted to go to her knees. She feared that would only release a wailing kind of prayer that would do none of them any good. Her travels in Europe with her parents, when her minister father had been highly revered, had given her quite an education. Especially in the kinds of illnesses that greed, poverty and cruelty inflicted on the innocent, destitute and helpless.

Her gaze locked with Brogan's. That brief sense of being inside each other's thoughts gave her comfort and strength that nearly brought tears to her eyes.

"Quarantine," she said, answering his silent questions. Breathing was difficult for a few heartbeats, under the weight of this understanding. He relied on her wisdom, her experience aiding the needy and sick, thanks to her childhood growing up with a traveling missionary society. "Willow bark tea to fight the fever. A warm bath with rosemary and peppermint oil to fight infection and help her breathe. Clean clothes. Several of those lovely herbal candles Mrs. Pettigrew has been creating. To cleanse the air and fight off the sickness. Then ..." She spread her hands, feeling a little helpless and hating it. "We will see what happens. What changes."

Ransom walked with them and shared the news swirling through the darker side of Cleveland's society. He had carried Mouse more than a dozen blocks to the Tower entrance, choosing the cold rather than risk exposing other tunnel dwellers to any sickness the girl might be carrying. The Tower entrance provided the shortest route to the place where Brogan and Ransom had arranged to meet. Despite the cold winds sucking away their warmth, Mouse's fever sweat had soaked through the blanket and Ransom's coat, and into his clothes. Common sense said he should wash thoroughly and change his clothes, to reduce risk of infection.

Carmen and Mary settled Mouse in a chamber set back from the main traffic patterns through the tunnels, with good ventilation directly outside, so no one else would breathe possibly infected air. Then they joined the two men in the kitchen. It was the heart of the community more than the meeting chambers, or the large bubble in the rock that had been dubbed the Chapel, with its wonderful acoustics for singing. Brogan had a ledger open on the table, and was sharpening a pencil with his penknife when the two women walked into the kitchen. Ransom's hair still looked damp from his bath, but curls lifted up all over his head in the warmth of the kitchen. His clothes looked a little large, and common sense said Brogan had loaned some of his to the slightly slimmer man.

"The cruel weather we've been having seems to have cut us off from much of the news we normally receive down here." Brogan gestured at his ledger. He flipped up a few pages as Carmen settled onto the bench next to him, showing just how much Ransom had been telling him and he had been recording. "I pray the Lord that proves true for this sickness, as well."

"How's the little gal?" Ransom asked.

"Like a rag doll." Mary shook her wrinkled, white head. "That one wasn't made to sit still." A snort escaped her, and she and Carmen exchanged crooked little smiles. "Washed at least a dozen layers of dirt off her while we were at it. Should do her some good. She was alert enough to protest the bath."

"Always a good sign," Brogan said.

"How truly bad is it, up above?" Carmen asked.

"I'm going to call in some favors to get information that Cleveland's officials are likely reluctant to release," Ransom said. "I swear, Miss Hilda's street sparrows know more about what's going on in this town than all the newspaper reporters and investigators and police officers put together. This weather is keeping people at home, so donations to shelters and other charity groups are falling off. The rumors of sickness are keeping more people at home if they can't leave the city. Of course, those who have the means to flee for their health are the very ones we depend on to donate food and clothing, fuel and now medicine, to make up the shortfall in the charity wards." He shrugged. "I already counted the situation worse than anyone is willing to admit, but I fear I have been optimistic."

"Somebody needs to warn Hilda," Mary said. "To protect her children, and to prepare for siege, when people are desperate enough to lose what little manners they have."

"I wouldn't doubt Miss Hilda knows already," Brogan said. "Maybe we should bring them all down here, the children and her workers and teachers, to protect them from exposure?"

"Ordinarily, I'd agree," Carmen said, "but tight conditions could spread this fever just as quickly as filth and starvation."

The original reason for Ransom coming down to the tunnels to meet with Brogan never came up in the conversation. That made sense, and Carmen didn't think about it until much later that evening, after the community gathered for dinner, and to discuss preparing for the holidays. The evening singing wasn't as spirited as usual, and none of the usual protests arose when it was time to send the children to bed. Carmen thought the news of Mouse being sick was to blame. The inquisitive, energetic orphan girl was the pet of many tunnel residents. So many of the rough, down-on-their-luck folk softened and brightened under the child's influence.

Carmen and Brogan went for a walk after the singing. By silent agreement, they picked up sacks and bushel baskets. Energy whispered through the crystal rose lying against her skin. Ahead, where the tunnel widened, a greenish-gold shimmer sparked into life at chin level in the air and grew, expanding to a soap bubble film that filled the tunnel. She and Brogan exchanged smiles of anticipation, and stepped through.

"Oh, glorious," Carmen whispered, as they stepped out into warm breezes scented with ripe apples and blackberries and the green smell of grass and leaves baking in a summer sun.

The mountainside stretched upward and downward, right and left, beyond the scope of their vision, in a constant noontime under an invisible sun. Carmen ached to simply drop to her knees and soak in the warmth and the fresh, clean, rich scents. Her regular escapes to the place she had dubbed Hidden Mountain made the constant damp and chill and darkness of the tunnel community bearable. That, and knowing she and Brogan would return with baskets and sacks full of fresh food to feed their people and give away to the truly destitute of Cleveland. The need to harvest kept her moving when she wanted to simply sit and indulge. Brogan smiled, then bent to pick up a bushel basket and three sacks. She took the other basket and remaining sacks, and they parted company for the next two hours.

At the end of that time, they had a sack full of walnuts and almonds. Two sacks of apples. A bushel basket of potatoes, another of carrots. A sack of cabbages and turnips. And a sack of oranges. Carmen took care picking the oranges, intending them for Mouse. She had heard and read good things about the benefits of citrus in fighting fevers and other illnesses.

"By spring, when we have people residing in the Tower, we'll be able to spread out farther, bring in a bigger harvest," Brogan said, when Carmen set down her sacks. He took off his jacket and spread it out on the ground a few steps away from the pile of bounty, waiting to go back to the tunnels. "I don't know how we can do it without raising too many questions, dangerous questions, maybe even bringing people snooping until they find us down here --" He chuckled. "Well, not here, here, but in the tunnels." He held out his hand and she let him help her settle on his jacket.

"But you envision being able to feed the entire city, if need be?" she asked.

"As you pointed out the first time we came here together, what use is it having this place, all this bounty, if we don't share it with those who need it?" He gestured around them, the groves and orchards and streams stretching as far as the eye could see. "The Lord made us able to find this time bubble, so we could help others. My fear is that if we aren't careful, our enemies could find it, and destroy it."

"My mother fled the Revisionists and took one of their greatest talents away from them, simply by deciding to follow her conscience. I have to believe they are crippled, and our soldiers continue to cripple them." Carmen slipped her hand into his. "With all the crystal we have brought through the light door, to hide here on the mountain ... eventually no one, either Originator or Revisionist, will have access to enough crystal to harm anyone."

"And the world will be safe from the folly of our ancestors, once the secret dies with us?" He chuckled when she made a face at his dire pronouncement. "My dear Songbird ... how can anyone lose hope when you are there to speak sense and faith to us all?" He twined his fingers through hers, so their palms pressed together.

Carmen shivered in an entirely pleasant way. She was sure her face was bright pink, but forgot that a moment later when a clear image flashed between their minds.

"Why does Mr. Wallace ... oh, of course." She laughed when Brogan's expression turned sour. All except the mischief in his eyes.

"I can see keeping secrets from you, good and bad, will be impossible soon," he grumbled.

"You and Mr. Wallace want to make a ring of crystal for Ess. He plans to propose marriage to her at Christmas. How lovely!" She evaded his gaze and tugged her hand free, so he wouldn't sense her momentary ache of envy. "You want my help to make a ring from crystal?"

"Your mother and Vivian Fremont fashioned their twin roses from crystal. If they could do it, surely you could find a way." He sighed, and his smile turned weary.

"Ess and I discussed this very problem. Several times." Carmen clasped her hands and bowed her head, hoping she feigned concentration, so he wouldn't guess the longing she couldn't quite repress. "We theorized that our mothers *sang* the crystal into the shape they wanted."

"Do you think you and I could sing crystal into a ring?"

"In theory." She forced herself to meet his gaze. "We will not know for certain until we try, will we?"

An hour later, she and Brogan had transferred their harvest through the light door and summoned helpers to haul the baskets and sacks to the kitchen. Carmen peeled an orange and took it to Mouse's sickroom. The little girl wasn't asleep. That had to be a sign she was improving already, because she was as much a nocturnal creature as her namesake. She smiled when Carmen brought her the pieces of orange, and struggled to sit up. Carmen worried when Mouse choked on the first bite of orange.

"Burns my throat," the girl explained when she got her breath back. That didn't stop her from devouring the fruit. She declared she felt much better, but fell asleep again before Carmen finished the second verse of the bedtime song.

<><><>

Ransom had promised to return the next evening with any new information he managed to gather, about the true conditions in Cleveland. He didn't return, being busy with a new investigation for Endicott, Lewis and MacDonald.

Hilda's school and shelter for street children, and her restaurant, were torched late in the afternoon. Ransom got to work tracking down witnesses while Endicott and half his people brought most of the children to shelter underground. Hilda was at a charity hospital, tending to three of her oldest boys. They had been injured fighting off the men who broke into the building through the schoolroom, and set the fire. Ten other children were at different locations where rescuers and welfare workers had taken them to shelter. Either they had been burned or had been soaked with water from the firefighters' pumper engine, and then froze in the brutal storm bearing down on Cleveland. Lewis and several junior investigators and clerks for the law firm were busy tracking down the children's whereabouts and conditions, intending to bring them underground, where they would be safe.

Everyone agreed that Revisionists were the most likely guilty parties.

The population of the underground community nearly doubled within the space of two hours. Housing arrangements were shuffled and rearranged. What had always seemed like more than enough didn't stretch far enough. Carmen caught herself a handful of times about to say they should send up above to Miss Hilda, to ask for spare clothing or dishes. They entirely ran out of soap, scrubbing the filth and stink of the fire off the children. The dormitory rooms were crammed from one wall to another, with children sharing cots and pallets on the floor. The single men and women gave up their small cell bedrooms to three and four children each.

The close quarters were a blessing when nightmares struck. There was always someone close by to cling to or offer comfort, as the children wept away the memories of the terror and the loss of the only safe haven they had known.

MacDonald arrived around two in the morning with Hilda and several children whom the authorities had reluctantly allowed to leave with her, on her promise that she had a place to take them. None of them should have been out in the sleet and heavy winds after what they had endured. However, they all had younger siblings, and Hilda judged that being with their brothers and sisters would be better for them than staying under a doctor's care.

Carmen and Mary and Hilda were all wobbling on their feet by the time they had the newcomers washed and fed and settled. Hilda refused to go to her bed, in Carmen and Mary's room, and insisted on joining the meeting in the kitchen. Carmen didn't care how it looked. She sat down next to Brogan and gladly leaned into his warmth and support as the long day caught up with her. Putting her head down on the table in the middle of the conversation sounded lovely. Still, she couldn't, wouldn't get up and go to bed. There was so much work to be done.

They calculated what they needed to bring down to the tunnels to make everyone comfortable, and where they might find it; beds and more clothing and other supplies. The weather would delay obtaining everything and bringing it down below. Hilda wanted to send at least twenty of her children to the farm up near Sandusky, run by two couples who had been part of the Fremont household years ago. The trip might have been fine in pleasant weather, but no one could predict how long the storm would last, or how much worse it would get. Plus Revisionists might be watching for large groups of children leaving the city. Their enemies might have targeted Hilda's school and shelter to help them find Originator safe houses and resources, by following the children.

"But how did they know you were part of the Originators?" Carmen asked.

Lewis had that answer. Some suspicious characters loitering near the law firm and the Tower construction site had prompted them to send a shipment of recovered crystal to Hilda's for safekeeping, until someone could cart it down to the tunnels. They had thought that would be safer than giving any hint that the Tower would contain more than airship docking and access to the new rail lines to be built in the spring. Between the bad weather and her messengers falling ill, Hilda hadn't sent the crystal away. Two more shipments had come to be stored in the long building that was now mostly smoking rubble, coated in ice. No one among the crew who delivered the shipments, or Hilda herself, was sensitive enough to the song of crystal to know how strong or loud it had grown. The small chests of crystal were gone from the hiding place under the floor. It was a good guess someone among the Revisionists heard the crystal song, followed it, torched the building, and took the crystal in the confusion.

Something shattered in Hilda. Carmen sensed it. She signaled Mary and they hurried her away from the kitchen before she broke down in front of everyone.

"No fool like an old fool," Hilda said, her voice strained from resisting sobs. She wrapped her arms around herself and shuddered on the edge of her cot in the bedroom.

"How were you to know?" Carmen paused in unbuckling Hilda's shoes, to look up at the elderly woman. "No, just think. Be honest with yourself," she insisted, when the woman opened her mouth to answer. "How were you to know? You did the best you could. Quite often, that's all any of us can do."

"But -- my children -- and crystal -- in the hands of those -- those murdering -- brutes!" She bent her head and let the tears drip.

Mary and Carmen got her out of her damp dress and petticoats and corset, and into a warm, dry nightgown, wrapped her in a robe and blanket, and propped her up against the wall with pillows. Carmen stayed with Hilda while Mary hurried down the passageways to the kitchen to bring her some chamomile tea.

"If only we could just ... just go. Far way," Hilda murmured. Her voice was raspy, like all her tears had drained her dry so she was filled with sand. "Take the children some place where they can finally be safe. If it isn't Fagan types, destroying their innocence for profit, it's those animals who want to rewrite history, even with so much proof of their ancestors' failures. We need to go to another land. But where on this planet can we really be safe?"

"Maybe not on Earth at all," Carmen offered with a weary smile.

"Ah, yes. Another world." She made a little choked sound and managed a pale smile in return. "Another time altogether. Our ancestors traveled through time. If only we could."

Carmen shivered and fought a slightly hysterical bubble of laughter as an idea filled her mind. Was she being an utter ninny to even think it? Or maybe she was a ninny because she hadn't thought of it sooner.

Despite all the grand plans she and Ess and the Fremonts had made, when they first discovered the key to traveling to Hidden Mountain, very few people so far had been gifted with crystal to help them sense and open the light door. There was always so much to do, and the sanctuary of the tunnel community needed protecting even more than Sanctuary had ever been. After all, Sanctuary had been infiltrated by Revisionists, and had been destroyed to keep its treasures and knowledge out of their hands.

Carmen supposed the ingrained need for secrecy and caution could be blamed for not thinking earlier of Hidden Mountain as the answer to their needs. Still, she thought she had been unusually dense and scatterbrained not to have considered all the possibilities before.

As soon as Mary returned with the chamomile tea, Carmen

excused herself. She left Hilda in Mary's care and hurried back to the meeting. More people had joined it, and to a man and woman, they all looked weary and wrinkled with worry, some expressions positively grim. She didn't say anything as she came into the room and stepped around the table, which had been expanded to accommodate everyone. Brogan looked up, alert, eyes wide, and met her gaze. She could almost laugh at the hope putting a flush in his cheeks, and this further proof of the merging of their minds.

"What is it?" Endicott said, glancing back and forth between them.

Brogan stood and gave his seat over to Carmen, then stepped up behind her chair. His hands on her shoulders increased the sense of his mind brushing against hers.

"Why can't we take the children to the mountain?" Carmen said. "It's warm, there's all that fresh food, streams full of clean water. I dare any sickness to follow them there. Ready access to all the healing herbs we could ever want. We don't have to worry about enough clothing for them, because it's summertime. They can run around barefoot in the grass all day if they want. And if the worst happens and the Revisionists find their way down here, the children will be safe no matter what happens."

Every head turned to Endicott, the de facto leader despite his insistence that Brogan be in charge. The elder lawyer sighed, sat back, and slowly nodded, his eyes hooded in thought.

"I'm sorry," Phyllis Mortimer ventured after several moments, while Endicott visibly worked through the proposal. "What mountain? And how far south is it, that it's summertime?"

That prompted a chuckle from Lewis, then from Brogan. Endicott's expression warmed with a weary smile. He still had smears of smoke char on his face and clothes.

"I'm sorry," Endicott said. "There has been so much going on, so many things to attend to. We should have brought all of you in on the secret, the gift from the Almighty, months ago."

He then explained, simply and briefly, how the light door had been discovered, leading to what Ess Fremont theorized was a bubble in time. Brogan had so much crystal embedded in his face, he was naturally attuned to its song and power. He had found the doorway and feared he might be losing his mind because no one else seemed to sense it. Then Carmen had come to the tunnel community and tripped through the doorway. They had found that by touching, creating a circuit of contact, they could bring others through the doorway. Anyone sensitive to crystal's song, who had crystal on them, could find the doorway and go through.

Several of those around the table laughed when Endicott explained that they had been sending all the recovered crystal they could obtain through the doorway, because it blocked crystal's song. Oswald McGuire admitted that they all just assumed it was being hidden in some particularly deep tunnels, far enough underground to mute the resonance. There was more laughter when they finally understood that the mountainside was the source of all the fresh food they had been receiving, and not some mysterious benefactor or ally with access to a greenhouse.

Everyone roused themselves enough to go down the tunnels to the nearest access point. The laughter among them was refreshing, when several people exclaimed at the sight of the shimmering film of light, spreading to fill the tunnel. They held hands in groups of four or five, and stepped through together, taking along those who couldn't see the light because they weren't wearing crystal.

"I think I'm rather selfish," Carmen admitted later, when the meeting ended and everyone had dispersed. "It was my idea, and yet I have this odd disquiet about everyone knowing about our lovely little retreat. It's not our secret anymore."

"The mountain goes on forever in all directions." Brogan patted her hand, tucked into the crook of his elbow. They walked slowly down the passageway to her quarters. "I doubt we'll have any trouble finding a new place to retreat, far enough away to feel quite alone." He chuckled. "I know how you feel, though."

"Are you --"

"Angry? Merciful Lord, no. Songbird, how could I be angry when you did such a wonderful thing for the children?" He brought them to a stop a few steps from her door. Light gleamed underneath the door, showing Hilda and Mary were still awake. "I can't wait to see the children running around, barefoot, splashing in the streams, climbing the trees. Bombing each other with berries. Getting muddy." His smile faded and that troubled light she hated to see touched his eyes. "As lovely as this sanctuary of ours is, as much good as it does for our children ... they aren't able to truly be children. Not in the darkness and damp and chill. On the mountain, they will."

<><><>

While a vicious storm settled down on top of Cleveland, summertime surrounded the children and those who went through the light door to oversee their care. Carmen changed her lessons with the children to focus on botany, to learn all about the plants that now surrounded them. Part of that was to keep the children out of trouble, such as plucking a berry that wasn't safe for eating or picking flowers that were poisonous. She combined their lessons with long hikes of exploration. Every child carried a basket or sack with them, for foraging. At the end of each hike, they spilled their bounty on the long trestle tables that marked the boundaries of Hilda's camp kitchen, and she taught them how to create amazing dishes from freshly picked ingredients.

Their sanctuary had one flaw: the lack of darkness. When or how would the children sleep, living in perpetual noontime? They resolved that problem by setting up tents, holding ten children each, with thick enough cloth to block out all the light and create nighttime inside. The children had great fun with their tent city.

Mouse had her own tent, set apart from the others until they could be sure she wasn't contagious. She seemed distrustful of the open space, but she liked sitting in the thick grass with bare legs and feet. Despite her fair hair and complexion, two days had her tanned to nearly the same shade of brown as her former constant coating of dirt. Carmen wore a bonnet when she hiked with the children for their lessons, but she also developed a healthy golden glow. Brogan teased her that she would have to use some silly, expensive face cream that promised a porcelain complexion, if she wanted to go above ground during the winter. People would look at her strangely, with the current color of her skin.

Not that any of them wanted to go above ground or venture into the city. Between the snow and constant bitter, fierce winds tearing through the city off the lake, the tunnel community was glad to stay in hiding. Stories came to them of people running out of fuel for heating their homes, because they were afraid to venture outdoors. Food became scarce. Angry, hungry people refused to believe shops had run out of supplies, and broke into them. Stories of the foreign sickness slithered through the city. Along with the food that was now harvested daily, with the help of the children, the tunnel dwellers processed medicines from the bounty of the mountainside and sent it above ground as quickly as they could. Only time would tell if their efforts made any real difference against the illness.

The children were barely settled when the illness struck among their allies above ground. They debated whether to bring the adults through to the mountain, house them in the tunnels, or leave them above ground. Three days after moving Hilda's charges to the mountain, Duncan Ross, fourteen years old, woke up with a raging fever and stumbled out of his tent in search of cold water. He fell into the stream and nearly drowned before he thought to call for help. Hilda heard him first, and she summoned Carmen and Tabitha before there was an outcry that could panic the other children. They managed to settle Duncan in a makeshift tent on the other side of Mouse's, before any other children woke. Three more children were discovered, shivering and sweating in their blankets. Carmen hesitated to step back through the light door to the tunnels, to report, but Brogan and the council needed to know.

"I think we should still keep the children separate from the adults," Endicott said, after the latest news on the spread of the sickness had been reported.

In the end, they agreed to turn the habitable remains of Hilda's building into a hospital for their friends. The law firm headed up the work to patch up the building where fire and efforts to stem the flames had broken through walls and roof. In short order, the ill were warmly housed. The more important task was to guard against people who would try to steal from the ill or oust them from their shelter, reasoning they were going to die anyway, so why waste the food and fuel on them? That was the growing attitude, as the sickness settled into its second week in the city.

Carmen wondered how many people would succumb to the mysterious sickness simply because they were afraid. Essentially, they would believe themselves into dying.

She blamed her own worries for not thinking clearly. By the fifth day on the mountainside, Mouse was on her feet again, moving a little slower than usual, and coughing infrequently. Duncan broke a sweat and seemed to have made a turn for the better. The other three children were still feverish and unable to eat more than a mouthful of porridge, or maybe a few wedges of orange at a time. Carmen sang to them and prayed over them and tried not to despair when the shimmers of energy from her crystal rose didn't seem to do them any good. How could it have healed Mouse's broken leg, yet failed to oust the sickness draining the children?

She needed the blue lotus, the keystone to controlling all the crystal brought into the past by the time-traveling ancestors. Why hadn't she thought of that first?

*Because,* she answered herself after thinking until her head hurt, *we are so sure we are superior to all the people around us, we think we can find any answer we need, fashion any remedy we want. We are unused to asking for help, I do fear.*

Carmen made sure she asked forgiveness for her complacency and arrogance, when she said her prayers that night. She focused on Ess Fremont, praying her friend would hear her in her dreams, through the connection forged by the crystal roses they both wore. If anyone could persuade the crew of the airship, the *Golden Nile,* to come to Cleveland earlier than planned, Ess could.

However, as hard as she tried to reach through her dreams and the rose that night, Carmen never got even an echo of the touch of Ess's mind. This was the worst possible time to learn the limits of crystal, and the communication link between their minds. Either the airship had gone far enough away that crystal's energy couldn't bridge the gap, or the mountainside was so utterly not of Earth that there was no bridge possible.

<><><>

"Idiot. I'm an idiot," she told Brogan, when he came to visit the children's camp the next morning.

"How?" He looked like he tried not to laugh at her. "Tell me what you should have done that you haven't done, or done wrong."

"I didn't think, that's what."

"You have a good excuse." He caught hold of her hand, and with his free hand gestured at the children spread around them.

The healthy children were several yards away, in the stream shallows, having a grand time splashing each other. Duncan was propped up in the shade of an awning, trying to read. Mouse wasn't allowed to get wet, but she crouched on the edge of the stream, cheering on her friends. It was an idyllic scene, yet Carmen couldn't shake her certainty a cloud would slide across the sky in another moment and cast them all into gloom.

"I could very well kick myself for not thinking to send the children through here earlier," Brogan added.

"I fear that living here rather ... separates us from the rest of the world. The real world, I suppose. I should be more aware of the passage of time, and yet ... when is the *Golden Nile* due?"

"Why do you ask?"

For a moment, Carmen just gaped. Of everyone, she thought Brogan would understand best. Then she realized she had never gotten far enough to tell him her idea. She couldn't decide whether to laugh at herself or crumple in mortification.

"The lotus." Half her trepidation died when Brogan's eyes widened and he nodded.

"Of course. If anything can heal the children, Athena and the blue lotus are our answer. Brilliant."

"Not so brilliant when I didn't think of it earlier. Do you know when they are due?"

Brogan wasn't sure. He was properly sympathetic when she related how she had tried to reach Ess through their dreams, but couldn't. He agreed that the time bubble holding the mountainside likely prevented that connection. He suggested Carmen spend that night in her quarters in the tunnels and try to reach Ess.

"That would be the sensible thing to do, but ... It's one thing to leave the Hilda and Mary along with the children long enough to deliver a new batch of medicine or more harvest, but overnight? I couldn't."

Brogan proposed that he find out when the airship was supposed to return to Cleveland. If the ship wasn't due for another week, then maybe Carmen should return to the tunnels, if that was what it took to contact Ess.

He returned only an hour later and led her on a long walk along the widest stream, to speak privately. He couldn't send a messenger to the law offices to ask if they had word of the airship. The usual runner among Hilda's street sparrows was among the sick children. Any number of tunnel residents were willing to go, but the fact that they were sheltering underground instead of working above ground made Brogan hesitate to ask. Several small riots had erupted throughout the city over the spreading sickness and the lack of supplies coming in. A prudent man stayed off the streets while such unrest grew. Brogan promised to send someone after dark, when the shadows would make the journey above ground a little safer.

As if the news of the small riots wasn't bad enough, Carmen was disconcerted to learn that the date wasn't what she thought. Two full days more had passed than she was aware of, since bringing the children here to the mountainside. Time itself passed differently within the time bubble of the mountainside, even with a pocket watch to accurately measure minutes and hours.

"We're almost to Christmas," she nearly wailed, when Brogan told her the date.

The dismay that widened his eyes brought a bubble of laughter from her. She regretted that, when he confessed that the tunnel community did little to celebrating or mark the holidays. Yes, they always made sure the children had treats, no matter how thin and boring the supplies might become in the winter. However, the thought of gathering the community together and worshipping as a body, singing, fellowshipping, even playing games, had never really occurred to them. They had shared memories of happier times, before enemies and sorrows and loss drove them to shelter underground, but no one even suggested they try to create their own traditions.

"We were content and felt ourselves fortunate," Brogan admitted, after some quiet moments with a furrowed brow and his gaze turned inward. "We all had lost so much, we thought we were rich enough, considering where we might have been." He shrugged. "Maybe we were afraid."

"Of what?" Carmen twined her arm with his and they paused on the bank of the stream.

"Being punished for ingratitude, I suppose." He squeezed her hand and interwove their fingers. "That will change, I promise. Christmas should be a celebration of gratitude, not a time of looking back at what used to be. Besides ..." His big, dark eyes twinkled. "We have five times as many children now. They outnumber us. Best to keep the natives happy."

Carmen had to laugh at that. She was still smiling, five hours later, when she stepped through the light door and went to meet Brogan and wait until the messenger returned from the law offices. A shimmering from crystal lingered in the air. It nicely counteracted the tunnel chill that had wrapped around her like a damp, threadbare blanket. Carmen followed the fading song of crystal, positive it would lead her to Brogan. No one else currently in the tunnels could sing to crystal and have it respond.

Unless the *Golden Nile* had showed up since Brogan had left the mountainside, and Ess had sung to the crystal to let her know she was there? Carmen picked up her pace and had to restrain herself from hurtling through the darkness too quickly. She could hit a wall or even lose her footing in the spots where the damp collected into puddles on the floor.

At the next branching of the tunnel, in the puddle of light from an oil lantern hung from the ceiling, she met up with Ransom Wallace.

Curiously, the shimmering lingered on him.

"Miss Mackenzie?" He held out a hand to her, frowning. "Are you all right?"

"You're ... well, you're echoing, I suppose." She remembered what she and Brogan had talked about, what felt like a lifetime ago. "Have you been exposed to crystal recently?" To her amusement, he blushed enough to be seen in the lantern light.

"Brogan is helping me with an experiment. Of sorts." He coughed, looked away, and gave the distinct impression he wanted to be far away, yet his good manners kept him there.

"You're trying to make a gift for Ess out of crystal, with Brogan's help, aren't you?" Carmen muffled a chuckle when his eyes widened and panic faded the blush. "Did you have any success?"

"Perhaps. He still has to -- we're experimenting."

"Carmen?" Brogan's voice slid down the winding passageway. A moment later, the crystal resonance grew stronger.

"What did the two of you do?" she called, pitching her voice to be heard. "Can you feel the crystal singing?"

Brogan laughed. "We sang to it until we couldn't hear it." A a soft glow of reflected lantern light appeared on the wall in the bend a dozen steps further down the tunnel. "We thought we had just ... I don't know, become attuned to it?"

"So attuned you can't tell you're humming." She rubbed her arms, feeling the hairs standing up against her sleeves. "This could be rather inconvenient, if you continue to sing in tune with the crystal, and lose the ability to hear it at the same time."

"If you'll excuse me, Miss Mackenzie," Ransom began.

"Oh, please, don't think I'll betray you to Ess. If you're making her a very special gift, you have my blessing." She patted his shoulder like she would one of her students.

"You have no idea ..." He swallowed loudly. He bowed and hurried into the darkness.

"Did you put the fear of God into our friend?" Brogan appeared at the bend in the tunnel. He laughed and picked up his pace.

"Are you making a ring for him to propose to Ess?"

Brogan stumbled. "Confound it, can't a man have any secrets around you?" Then he tipped his head back and laughed.

They went to his office and workshop. Ransom had promised to check if there was any news about the *Golden Nile*. Brogan wanted to show Carmen what he and Ransom had been doing. Essentially, they had been experimenting with bits and pieces of crystal. Just as she had theorized with him earlier, singing did reshape the crystal, but Brogan needed to invest many long hours to gain the finesse to create the desired outcome.

"One interesting detail we've learned so far," he said, after showing her several pieces of crystal that looked melted, like a candle set too close to the gas stove. "Crystal doesn't like other crystal." He cupped several pieces of crystal in his hands and shook them together, giving off chords that changed as the pieces bounced off each other. The notes lingered, so chord built on chord, sending pleasant trills up Carmen's spine.

"What?" She laughed at the sensation that the music sank through her flesh. An odd feeling of mixed disappointment and relief wrapped heavy around her chest, as the chords faded. She wanted it to continue. Was this what it was like for the men and women she had seen caught in opium dens? "How can crystal feel anything?"

"That isn't the right word, and yet I don't know what is." He settled back in his usual chair and smiled a little wearily at her. "We thought to be economical and merge several small pieces together, to make the engagement ring. Even try to twist several colors together. There are some fragments with tints of blue and lavender. I sang myself nearly hoarse, and no matter how soft the crystal grew, no matter how adept we both were at prodding it with wooden rods to create shapes while it was soft, the pieces would not bond. We even tried braiding them together. They repelled each other like similarly charged magnetic poles."

"Fascinating," she murmured. "So you have a new challenge. Finding a single piece that isn't too large for a suitable ring."

"Essentially." He nodded. "Would you mind too much giving me a few hours each afternoon, to experiment more?"

"To make sure Ess has a ring? I would not mind in the least." She fought back another chuckle at the relief brightening his face. What was worrying the man? Could his long-ago injury caused by crystal make him uncomfortable with this task? Perhaps he experienced the same addictive tug she had felt, and wanted her help to keep him from falling under crystal's influence. "In fact, I insist on being part of this."

<><><>

Ransom returned barely two hours later, with gifts and surprises to transport to the mountainside. Brogan excused himself almost immediately, saying a security issue had arisen. Carmen barely noticed in all the excitement. Tomas, Peggety, Waldo and Bridget had come from the farm near Sandusky. They had been part of the Fremont household when Ess was growing up. Since Hilda couldn't come to them for Christmas, and the Fremonts were delayed in arriving in Cleveland, they had decided to come here. They brought all sorts of provisions, including new clothes for the children's Christmas presents, hams and sausages, barrels of flour and sugar, and spices for Christmas baking.

They also brought a tree for decorating. Tomas and Waldo sighed and shook their heads when they came through the light door and saw the cluster of pines less than ten minutes of walking away from the meadow containing the tent village.

"Men." Bridget exchanged exasperated looks with Peggety and Hilda, which fractured quickly into smiles, then laughter. "There's a huge difference between a tree that just stands there, and a tree specially cut down for decorating and celebrating."

"Aye," Tomas said. "My achin' muscles and pine tar on my clothes." He chuckled and sidestepped when she made to swat at him.

"Hush now." Hilda gestured at the tents. "It's hard enough getting the little ones to sleep when it's perpetual noontime here.

Don't go waking them." She tipped her head to one side and regarded Carmen a moment. "I suppose this seems like foolishness to you, but it's a tradition Matilda and Ernest started after a stay in England. They picked it up from the academic folk they were socializing with, and they picked it up in turn from Prince Albert. Seems a mighty fine tradition, those Germans have. Gives some brightness to some cold, gloomy winter days."

"Oh, no, I wasn't confused, or criticizing. I was just remembering …" Carmen sighed and blinked away the first hot threat of memory tears. "My parents and I spent some time in England and Germany, when I was younger. In the glory days, when my father was quite in demand as a preacher. Christmas decorations and the tree are some of my brightest memories. This was a very good idea. The children will adore it."

"Oh, I'm glad." A chuckle escaped her. "You can be in charge of figuring out decorations. It's a given that candles will be useless, with all this lovely sunshine." She tipped her head back and searched the sky, as if still trying to pinpoint the invisible sun.

Once all the provisions had been settled under the canopy that marked the kitchen area, Carmen took Ransom back through the light door. Waldo and Tomas were marking out an area where they wanted to build a beehive oven for baking.

The fading chords of crystal song greeted them. Carmen caught her breath, for a moment torn between simply closing her eyes to indulge in the music, and bracing to resist the allure.

"What is that?" Ransom whispered.

"You heard that?" She reached out to press her hand against the nearest tunnel wall. Sure enough, the stone hummed with the song. He copied her and his eyes widened. "That is crystal."

"I'm not one of you, so how can I hear it now?"

"Well, I would guess exposure … tunes you to it? You spent how long with Brogan, playing with the shards earlier?"

"Well, that's interesting." He pursed his lips in thought and slowly nodded. Excitement gleamed in his eyes, making her laugh.

"One more thing you and Ess will have in common." She patted his shoulder. "Let's test this new sensitivity of yours. Can you follow it to where Brogan has been working?"

The chimes and chords had faded sufficiently by the time they were halfway to Brogan's office that Ransom no longer felt the shimmering in air and stone. Not that they needed any guidance. In those few minutes of walking, Carmen had time to wonder why Brogan would work on the crystal when she wasn't there. Hadn't he asked for her help in singing the crystal into the desired shape?

"Well, that's an interesting development," Brogan greeted them, as he appeared in the doorway of his office. They were still a good dozen steps down the passageway. "I could feel you coming. Well, more accurately, I felt your crystal rose. Perhaps I am overtired, but I think the song changes, depending on the amount of crystal on the person in question." He bowed, with a wicked twist of humor in his lips and gleaming in his eyes. "You have a musical signature all your own, Miss Carmen."

"No doubt I could say the same for you, Mister Brogan Ambrose," she returned, with a brief pause to bob a curtsey.

"Any progress?" Ransom asked.

"Hmm ..." Brogan eyed her, then stepped back into his office, gesturing for them to come in. "I was experimenting, let's say. Testing some new theories."

"Boss." McTeague skidded through the doorway, nearly running into Ransom. "Sorry, but they're back." He nodded to Carmen, tugging on his cap, before dashing out again.

"Who is back?" she asked.

Brogan cursed under his breath and his features hardened as he stepped around her, to follow McTeague.

"I'm guessing your nasty friends," Ransom said. "Time to get back to work, I suspect. Good night, Miss Mackenzie." He nodded to her.

"Mr. Wallace." She repressed a sigh and moved over to her usual chair, intending to wait until Brogan came back.

Who else could "they" be, but more Revisionist hunters, trying to locate the Originator stronghold? After all that trouble this past summer with Richard Boniface, the Revisionists had to at least suspect the Originators had an outpost of some kind here in Cleveland. Despite all the successes they had enjoyed, capturing the spies and ensuring no communication went back to the Revisionist leaders, they really couldn't be sure some information, some clue, didn't remain to someday lead their ancestral enemies back here.

Carmen sighed, too weary to laugh at the irony in her thinking.

Her mother, Anna, had been a Revisionist, and strong in the ability to handle and even control crystal. She had decided the Revisionists were wrong, and had fled, harming their cause by depriving them of her talents. Fortunately, she had encountered Vivian Fremont, part of a powerful Originator family. Vivian believed her desire to change allegiance and had helped Anna hide. Their friendship enabled them to sing crystal into the twin roses that they had used to communicate. Carmen and Ess had been childhood friends, linked by their mothers' roses, then separated by their mothers' deaths. Reunited, they had dealt the Revisionists a powerful blow.

Total defeat of the Revisionists and their mission would not come until all the crystal pieces of the two time-traveling machines had been found and taken out of their reach. Through the light door. Evil was strong and persistent. The Revisionists' ancestors had tried to rewrite history by trying to prevent Bethlehem or Calvary. The ancestors of the Originators had flung themselves into the time stream to prevent it. The Revisionists would keep hunting for crystal until it was taken out of their reach, so even the most sensitive of their hunters couldn't feel its song.

Carmen paused as that thought reverberated through her mind. Muffling a cry of anguish, she hurried out of Brogan's office and went in search of him.

She found him with more than a dozen of the men who served as sentinels, guarding the various doorways from the surface down into the tunnels. The room was another cellar, all that remained of a building that had been torn down as Cleveland continued to grow and expand along the shore of Lake Erie. It was separated from the tunnels, but used as a drop point for supplies and messages. Carmen had to go above ground and walk down an alley, to the next street, then enter a warehouse and take another tunnel to the cellar. She was grateful for the alley that kept most of the snow off her on the short walk. Brogan would scold her for going outside in the freezing weather without more than a shawl.

Brogan stayed at the edge of the puddle of lantern light, allowing Begley, the leader of the sentinels, to deal with two men who sat tied back-to-back on a crate. Carmen stayed in shadows of the crooked doorway of the cellar. No one seemed to notice her entrance but Brogan, who turned to glance her way. The crystal embedded in his face had likely responded to the presence of her rose and warned him. She couldn't see his expression, but she saw him shake his head. Yes, she should have waited for him at the tunnel entrance. It wasn't like she could tell him here and now what she had discovered.

He said something she couldn't catch, and Begley stepped over to him, holding out what looked like a dirty handkerchief. Crystal song whispered across her skin the moment the handkerchief touched Brogan's hand. He crossed the darkness to her side, hooked his arm through hers, and led her back up the broken stairs, through the warehouse. They were silent until they returned down the alley and were safely in the tunnels again.

"The Revisionists heard when you were working with the crystal," Carmen said, the moment Brogan took a deep breath. She could feel him bracing to scold her. She adored him right that moment, knowing how much he didn't want to be angry with her. "That's what brought them. Isn't it?"

"I fear so. Which begs the question of whether it is safe for Ransom to give his ladylove a ring of crystal, for their engagement." He snorted. "If he ever gets up the courage to ask her."

"If he's a wise man, he will." She let out a sigh as the tension drained out of her. "Ess is strong enough to keep the song quiet. No one can tell when she's wearing crystal unless she's using it."

"Hmm. That's some comfort, I suppose. Is she as strong as you, would you think? Or stronger?"

"She has more training than me, but Matilda thinks I have more inborn control. If we could only have more time to train together, she says we will make quite a formidable team someday. Maybe even stronger than all the women who sang the Great Machine apart when the ancestors first came through time."

"That's a comforting thought." He patted her hand, tucked as usual in the crook of his elbow.

"Is the ring finished?"

"It bloody well has to be now, doesn't it?" He sighed. "Forgive me, Songbird. Facing down those vile … well, they'll get no chance to report to their superiors. Begley has a talent for tricking men into revealing more than they thought they knew. Building the Tower is almost like sending up a flare for our enemies. Here we are, come get us if you can. At the same time, when it is finished, it will be a fortress, another barrier over us."

"The sooner we have all the crystal in the world through the door and hidden on the mountain, the better the entire world will be. They can't hear --" She laughed.

"I am sorely in need of some good news. Please share what amuses you."

"Well, you can come to the mountain to finish the ring. What could be a safer workplace?"

"Hmm, yes, with Mouse and all the others gathered around, asking a dozen questions a minute, making it impossible to concentrate on my task." In the glow from the lantern ahead of them, she saw him smile. "Very good idea. I should have thought of it sooner."

"We both should." Carmen tipped her head to rest, just a little, against his shoulder as they walked.

The dirty handkerchief, she found out a short time later, held a short rod of crystal, similar to the rods some Originators carried. Someone among the new prisoners had enough sensitivity to strike the rod and follow the responding shimmer of crystal energy to its source. She felt a brief satisfaction when Brogan entrusted the rod to her, to take through the light doorway and permanently out of the hands of their enemies.

<><><>

Just as Brogan expected, the children were fascinated with watching him and Carmen work with the crystal. They gathered around, unusually silent when the singing began and the crystal glowed and gave off different soft, pastel colors. Some of the children pressed their hands to their temples or cupped their ears, indicating they heard more than the others did. Carmen made special note of them.

Mouse, of course, had the idea to use the bits of crystal to decorate the Christmas tree. She had heard Hilda and Peggety sighing over the fact that they couldn't have candles on the tree, simply because they wouldn't make any difference in the constant noontime light. Crystal, however, gave off rainbows that changed as the breeze moved the branches.

They had a grand time, decorating the tree with bits of crystal held in loose nets of thread hung on the tips of the branches. Carmen told the children about Martin Luther starting the tradition, to bring the stars indoors to celebrate the holy season, and then Prince Albert introducing the tradition in England after marrying Queen Victoria. She and Hilda told stories about the trees they had seen when they had both lived in England and Germany, years ago. The children were enchanted with their tree, and several discovered to their delight that if they sang Christmas hymns to the tree, the crystals glowed and the rainbows grew brighter for minutes at a time.

The only sour note in that lovely afternoon of stories and singing and stringing popcorn came from Carmen herself. She scolded herself several times not to be so selfish, but she couldn't quite repress little twinges of jealousy. Ess would be delighted with the ring when Ransom gave it to her -- if the *Golden Nile* ever reached Cleveland. Brogan came up with four ring designs, with her help. One was a simple, smooth, flat band. One was a round band. One had a spiral worked into the crystal, and the fourth was the most lovely of them all, in Carmen's estimation. After nearly half an hour of experimenting, she and Brogan sang a piece of crystal into a long strand they temporarily separated into three pieces, then quickly braided, then coaxed into a ring. When they stopped singing, each strand remained distinct and maintained a different shade -- lavender, pale blue, and clear.

Carmen fought not to reveal how much she liked that ring, and the strangely painful longing for Brogan to offer it to her. She tried not to be angry with him, when he had her try it on, and then asked her if she was sure she and Ess had the same size hands.

"No matter how clever he is, he is a man, after all," she consoled herself that evening, when the children had been coaxed through the washing battle and sent to bed several times each. They were excited about their tree, after all, and kept trying to slip out of their tents to look at it again. "No matter how wonderful they are, sometimes they are quite oblivious to what is directly under their noses."

Christmas Eve, Brogan suggested if the weather stayed friendly, they try to attend the midnight service at the Old Stone Church. Carmen was so stunned at the very idea of him voluntarily going out in public, she said yes without thinking. Then she thought of leaving Hilda and the others to take care of the children. Brogan laughed at her as she stumbled through trying to back out of the invitation without backing out. She chose to laugh with him instead of being perturbed, when he revealed that he had already made sure she could be free of her responsibilities for a few hours. After all, despite their excitement and the difference in time between the mountainside and the tunnels, the children would be asleep by the time she left to walk across Public Square with him. Granted, there was no guarantee they would sleep through the night. She would simply have to trust that not all of them would wake at the same time.

Snow dusted the air when they came above ground and set off down the side streets, with the river and the slowly growing Tower behind them. No wind blew, and that took the bite off the ever-present frigid dryness of the air. Carmen was quite content to walk silently, arm-in-arm with Brogan, surrounded by nearly two dozen other tunnel residents who thought it was a fine idea to bring in Christmas day in worship. The gaslight shining through the thin stained glass panels in the front of the church beckoned them through the lacy white sifting through the air, and the lamps trimming the square quite gave the scene a Currier and Ives feeling.

Despite the cold and the constant fear of another snowstorm paralyzing the city, the church was nearly three-quarters filled when their group arrived. Fortunately, everyone wanted to sit up near the front and along the sides, where small portable coal and oil stoves radiated warmth. That left plenty of room in the back and along the center aisle for their party to sit in shadows, safe from the gaslight. Brogan removed his hat when they entered the sanctuary, but he left his scarf wrapped up high around his ears, covering most of his scarring. Carmen thought about teasing him about vanity, because it was quite invisible in the shadows. Or perhaps she would tease him about muffling his voice during the singing portion of the service.

She forgot that, when they stood to sing the first song. Crystal sang through the air, surrounding her. She nearly forgot herself and turned to look around. She had never felt it so strong in the air before. Was it some reaction to the holy surroundings of the church? Or had someone else come in wearing crystal? Could they have been followed to church by a Revisionist, following echoes of crystal song? Brogan caught hold of her hand, and that intensified the sensation of the shimmering music, through both their pairs of knit gloves.

"Ransom is here," he whispered, when the minister announced the next song the congregation would sing.

Carmen nearly laughed aloud, and called herself a fool. She thought about sharing with him her thoughts, later. He would laugh if she remarked that she didn't think a Revisionist could step foot on holy ground without bursting into flame. When the song finished, she had a moment to look around while everyone sat down. Ransom Wallace sat on the other side of the aisle, one row back. He nodded to her and smiled, and she smiled back. She felt a little sorry for him, carrying the crystal ring when no word had come yet of the *Golden Nile*'s expected arrival.

Or perhaps he did have word, and did have hope the airship carrying the Fremonts would arrive for Christmas Day? An engagement at Christmas sounded lovely, rather sentimental. Something to remember for years to come.

A sigh escaped her, echoed in an increased shimmering of the crystal rose against her skin. Carmen sat up straighter and scolded herself for having so little control, especially in church. She took a breath and braced herself for the effort to silence the crystal. Truthfully, she should be ashamed at how little time she had devoted to the discipline exercises Matilda had given her. What good did it do her to have so much more inherent strength and talent with crystal than Ess if she employed no discipline?

*High time you thought of me,* Ess said in her mind. *Where has your mind been lately?* Laughter trickled through their connection.

*Are you here?* Carmen squeezed Brogan's hand, which hadn't released hers since the singing.

*Just tying up the* Nile *now. I'm half-minded to take one of the descent ropes instead of waiting for the basket with Granny and Grandfather.*

"Ess is here," she whispered to Brogan, when he bent his head down to almost touch his forehead to hers. *We're at church. I highly recommend the rope, even if you're wearing skirts. Mr. Wallace is practically tied up in knots, waiting for you.*

*Is he now?* Ess laughed. *We'll come to meet you, though the service will probably be over by the time we get there.*

Ordinarily, Carmen would be highly disappointed in a minister who barely spent fifteen minutes on the Christmas Eve homily, but tonight she was grateful. The moment the last note of the final hymn rang out, she tugged on Brogan's hand and stepped out into the aisle. She gestured with a tip of her head to Ransom as they headed for the back of the church, with the minister's final blessing to the congregation ringing through the air.

"What is it?" Ransom asked, as soon as the big wooden, brass-bound doors thudded softly closed behind them.

For answer, Carmen pointed. The air had cleared enough that the dark, oval outline of the *Golden Nile* was visible above the buildings on the other side of Public Square. Soft, tiny spots of light ringed the airship, making it visible at night. With so much increase in airship traffic, federal and municipal authorities had been busy passing laws requiring running lights when any air vehicle came within two miles of large cities and ports.

Ransom paused for several heartbeats on the top step, mouth falling open and then stretching wide in a grin. His shoulders straightened as if a heavy weight had fallen off them. He thrust his right hand into his coat pocket. Carmen knew he wouldn't take it out until he met up with Ess and could open the little wooden box filled with cotton, where the crystal ring nestled. He turned to her and Brogan, and his smile twitched a little. He nodded to them, then set off down the stairs and straight across Public Square, with no regard for sidewalks or snowdrifts or the ruts in the ice and frozen sludge carved by wagon wheels.

"Moment of truth," Brogan murmured.

"You're a horrible man, Brogan Ambrose," she retorted with a bubble of laughter thickening her voice. She let him loop her arm through his, and they started down the steps together at a more sedate pace. "I'd like to see how you will handle that moment, when it finally comes for you," escaped her lips before she had time to think.

"Would you, now?" He flinched when the doors creaked open behind them and the congregation began to slip out of the warm church into the frosty night.

"Oh -- I'm sorry -- that was quite -- It's been a long, weary day. The children are so excited --" A squeak escaped her when Brogan pressed two gloved fingers to her lips.

Laughter sparkled in his eyes, clear despite the shadows, as he led her down the sidewalk a ways, so they were out of the paths of those leaving the church, heading for waiting carriages and steamcarts.

"Miss Mackenzie -- Carmen -- dearest Songbird." He sighed and turned her to face him, and held both her hands. "I am quite irritated with Ransom, though I don't blame him, after all the waiting and not knowing and ..." Another sigh. "Our friend is stealing my thunder."

"Thunder?"

"Will you forgive me, torturing you as I did the other day?"

"How did you torture me?" Carmen shivered deep inside, so she could barely get enough breath to speak. Despite that, her words slipped out easily, as if someone else were speaking for her.

"I wanted to be sure. Confound it, I was a coward. I should have asked you to marry me right then, with the ring on your finger, but I wanted something beautiful for your memories. Our memories." His voice cracked and he looked away.

It struck her then that it was odd no one in their party had rejoined them in front of the church. They were quite alone, with everyone walking away in the other direction. Carmen caught her breath as understanding washed over her, warm and then cold and then bubbling up in laughter.

*This was all planned ...*

If they weren't out in public, and if the frustrating, darling man had tried at least once to kiss her, Carmen thought she might just grab the lapels of his coat and pull herself up to his level and kiss him. Wouldn't that astound him and shock him and pay him back for, yes, the torture he had put her through? She was just as much a coward as him.

"Yes, you're right." She laughed when his head nearly snapped back to face her and his eyes widened in something like panic. "You should have asked me then, and yes, this is a beautiful memory. You weren't planning on kneeling, were you? It's quite messy here."

Brogan laughed, a hearty bark of sound that echoed off the stone face of the church and other nearby buildings, despite the muffling of the thickening snow.

"I adore you, Songbird. Please, say you will spend the rest of your life with me, making music and brightening our dark kingdom?"

For a moment, she couldn't make a sound. Her voice cracked as she squeaked out her "yes," so she nodded to make sure he understood. This time his laughter was a roar as he wrapped his arms around her and lifted her up, to spin them around twice. She felt the flare of crystal in his coat breast pocket, and it quite took her breath away.

Brogan set her down and held her against his side, one arm tight around her while the other hand dug in his inner coat pocket. He brought out a little silken pouch. She recognized it with a sudden burst of happy, sentimental tears. Mouse had made that pouch for him, when she had been sick enough to stay in bed for an entire day and willingly take sewing lessons from Hilda. Carmen's hands shook as she struggled to slide off one glove. Even in the shadows, the ring sparkled when Brogan took it out of the pouch, and the glow grew as he slipped the braided crystal ring on her finger.

A bright flash erupted from the ring. Carmen had a momentary image of Ransom Wallace, down on one knee at the curb on the other side of Public Square, sliding a ring -- she wasn't sure which one, and she quite didn't care -- on Ess Fremont's finger. With a happy bubble of laughter, Carmen shut down the link between her and her once-imaginary friend. This was one moment she didn't want to share with anyone but Brogan.

# Christmas memories

One of our traditions growing up was the pizza and homemade Italian cookies that Aunt Anna – my father's aunt – would make and bring around to all the relatives on our grandparents' side of the family for Christmas. It just wasn't Christmas without a slice of fresh, homemade pizza, usually eaten cold. Nothing on it but the tomato sauce full of herbs, all sorts of specks of green and brown floating in a red sea of sauce.

Grandma always went all out with a formal dinner: lasagna, then city chicken and salad and vegetables, with little side dishes of provolone and green cracked olives and anchovies. We would sit around the big dining room table and play Bingo and other old games, until my brothers got very antsy, wanting to open presents. (This was when we were all in elementary school and junior high, so grant them some slack.) We would munch on the pizza and cookies later after we opened our presents.

When we got older and traditions changed and we became the hosts instead of going to our grandparents' house for Christmas Eve, we transitioned from the fancy dinner Grandma used to make to soup and pizza for Christmas Eve dinner. We'd buy several boxes of pizza and have the rest of the pizza for lunch Christmas day.

Nope, I'm not going to hand out Aunt Anna's pizza recipe, but here's a way for you to have your own, custom-made individual pizzas, with a lot less fuss. Depending on just how much you like to splurge on your pizza…

Start with **a jar of garlic and basil spaghetti sauce**. Go ahead, get the expensive kind. It's Christmas!
*If you're allergic to tomatoes, use a white alfredo sauce.*

Split and lightly toast **English muffins**, just enough they start to get golden. Have at least 2 per person. But seriously, you might want to provide 4 per person.

Spread a nice generous spoon of sauce on the lightly toasted English muffins, spread out on a broiler pan or a cookie sheet. Get the sauce to the edges, so they're covered.

**Toppings:**

- ✓ Shredded mozzarella
- ✓ Sliced pepperoni
- ✓ Cooked chunks of sausage -- Italian sausage, of course
- ✓ Cooked green pepper chunks. Big chunks. They taste better.
- ✓ Cooked rings of onion. Sweet onion.
- ✓ Sliced canned mushrooms. Sure, you can use fresh, raw mushrooms, but you're going to want them cooked a little bit, so save yourself time and get the canned ones.
- ✓ Sweet bell pepper rings
- ✓ Sliced black olives
- ✓ Sliced green olives

These are just the standard toppings. Remember, these are English muffins, so you don't have a lot of room to work with, but go ahead, pile the toppings high. It's Christmas!

**Suggestion:**
*Margherita pizza:* a slice of fresh tomato, then fresh basil leaves, then a thick slice of buffalo mozzarella

You can put other toppings on your pizza, if you're into the variations like Hawaiian or Mexican. There's a joke about a pizza parlor run by Andorians, from Star Trek fandom, but believe me, you don't want to eat the Andorian version of pizza. It's just … not … right.

Once you have your toppings piled on your English muffins, sprinkle with the **shredded mozzarella.** Then **broil** until the cheese melts and starts to turn light brown.

And you're done. Enjoy and repeat. It's Christmas!

And if you've got a really good Italian bakery or Italian grocery store nearby, please do indulge in some cookies for dessert. Especially the ones with almond flavoring in the dough and dipped in bittersweet chocolate and then slivered almonds. Yummy!

Find Michelle L. Levigne online:

***Website: www.Mlevigne.com***
***Blog: www.MichelleLevigne.blogspot.com***
***Twitter: @MichelleLevigne***
***Facebook: https://www.facebook.com/michelle.levigne.7***
***Or https://www.facebook.com/Michelle-Levigne-Author-and-Editor-73679232010/***

# THANK YOU!

Thank you for reading this book from Mt. Zion Ridge Press.

If you enjoyed the experience, learned something, gained a new perspective, or made new friends through story, could you do us a favor and write a review on Goodreads or wherever you bought the book?

Thanks! We and our authors appreciate it.

We invite you to visit our website, MtZionRidgePress.com, and explore other titles in fiction and non-fiction. We always have something coming up that's new and off the beaten path.

And please check out our podcast, **Books on the Ridge,** where we chat with our authors and give them a chance to share what was in their hearts while they wrote their book, as well as fun anecdotes and glimpses into their lives and experiences and the writing process. And we always discuss a very important topic: *Tea!*

You can listen to the podcast on our website or find it at most of the usual places where podcasts are available online. Please subscribe so you don't miss a single episode!

***Thanks for reading. We hope to see you again soon!***

www.ingramcontent.com/pod-product-compliance
Lightning Source LLC
Chambersburg PA
CBHW010358310726
48979CB00006B/1079

* 9 7 8 1 9 5 5 8 3 8 8 1 8 *